CHOKING ON THE
SPLINTERS

JIM LIVELY

TREATY OAK PUBLISHERS

Publisher's Note

**Printed and published in
the United States of America**

Treaty Oak Publishers

ISBN · 978-1-943658-89-3

also by Jim Lively

Aberrant Behavior
Punitive damages
The Puzzle Aesthetic
Surreal Absurdity

Available on Amazon

DEDICATION

In memory of my brother, John.

Chapter 1

Sanders turned fifty-five years old today. For fifty-five years, he had gone by his given name Charles, one he detested for fifty-five years. He went to school for nineteen years, practiced law for twenty-nine years, and was married for thirty-one years. Sanders no longer went to school, practiced law, nor was married. The precedent was established.

From this day forward, he would go only by his middle name of Sanders and his last name Pierce. Sanders was determined that changing his name was going to be just the beginning of a lot of changes in his life. He surmised that he was becoming too reclusive. While Sanders had a small group of fiercely loyal friends, he socialized with them less and less. After the death of his wife, four years ago, his dates with women bordered on the sporadic.

On his fifty-fifth birthday, Sanders was intent on making some dramatic life changes. The afternoon of his birthday, he spent researching dating sites. He had an aversion to the whole concept of finding a significant other on the web. However, several friends raved about the successes they had experienced.

He read review after review and at last settled on Nonpareil Match. Nonpareil was not the highest rated, but Sanders thought the name was clever and hit the 'join' tab. He reviewed the various options that one could select for enrollment purposes.

If I'm going to go down this path, I might as well go with the most expensive option!

Right away Sanders received a prompt to set up his profile. He completed the minimum required with the intention of finishing the rest of it later. Instead, Sanders began searching for all the eligible women from age thirty to sixty. He added a few search filters to further reduce the number of potential candidates. Some of the potential candidates invested more time than others in completing their profile and interests.

Sanders ignored those that failed to include at least one picture or those who fleshed out their profile to a bare minimum.

He was not interested in reaching out to anyone at this stage. The sole purpose of this exercise was due diligence. What were the features that made one's profile stand out?

A quick research indicated that men enrolled in Nonpareil exceeded the number of women by a two to one margin. Charles checked the time. It was 6:00 p.m. and he had a dinner engagement with a friend at Neighborhood Services on Beltline.

Neighborhood Services was an upscale American bistro. The owner was searching for a name for his soon-to-be-opened restaurant. A city of Dallas generic building permit described the new occupant as 'neighborhood services'. The new owner thought that was prophetic and the description became the restaurant's name.

There was just enough time to for Charles to change clothes and drive in the post rush hour traffic to the restaurant. He arrived at 6:55 p.m. and opened the door to the restaurant and scanned the restaurant for his friend, Gayle. She was an attorney who specialized in the same area of the law as Sanders before he retired from his practice.

Gayle was nowhere in sight, so Sanders made his way to the crowded bar and found an unoccupied stool. He ordered a cocktail and checked his phone to see if Gayle had tried to text him. Before he could put his phone back into his pocket, he felt a hand on his left shoulder.

A voice said, "I thought I might find you at the bar. Happy Birthday, old friend!"

Sanders spun around on his stool. "Thank you, Gayle! I'm so happy to see you. I was beginning to wonder if you were going to stand me up."

"My God, Sanders, I'm only five minutes late and you know me well enough, that five minutes late is the same as being on time."

Sanders laughed. "Fifteen minutes late for you is the same thing as being on time."

GAYLE SAID, "SO CHARLES…" She covered her mouth with her right hand in a playful gesture. "Sorry, Sanders. I'm having trouble getting use to calling you Sanders. After all, I've called you Charles for over twenty years."

"No problem, Gayle. You're grandfathered in for using Charles if you prefer."

Gayle smiled. "No, it's Sanders from now on. Shall we get a table?"

Sanders stood up. "Yes, I made a reservation so we should be seated pretty quickly."

The manager of Neighborhood Services recognized Sanders and seated them near the windows in a booth he knew Sanders preferred. After ordering dinner and a glass of wine, Sanders said, "How's the practice going?"

"It's going fine. I'm so glad I left the firm to go out on my own. Most of my clients followed me and yet I'm only having to work fifty hours a week instead of seventy."

Sanders smirked. "What do you do with all that spare time you have on your hands?"

Gayle leaned back in her chair. "I use it to get home at a reasonable time in the evenings and occasionally get to have dinner with old friends like you, Sanders."

"Well, I do thank you for joining me tonight."

"Tell me Sanders, what's going on with you? Are you still enjoying the life of an artist?"

Sanders grimaced. "Yes, but I'm afraid I've become a little too reclusive. Ever since I moved my studio from the Design District to the Core District in Richardson, I often don't have any social interaction during the day."

"Why did you move?"

"I was a sub-tenant in the Design District. When my landlord's rent was raised, she had no choice but to raise mine as well. When I went into art, I made a promise to myself that my art sales had to, at a minimum, pay for my art related expenses. I couldn't remain in the Design District and break even. I didn't think it was prudent to use savings to fund my art."

Gayle took a sip of wine. "Is the rent more affordable in the Core District?"

"Yes, by far. However, I'm not renting. I purchased the building as an investment. The former owner said he recently rented it to several photographers who broke their lease. The building has some unusual features though."

Gayle rested her elbows on the table. "Such as what?"

"All the windows were heavily tinted, which I guess is consistent with the use for photography. However, there are also all these diverted electrical lines attached to several large circuit breakers. One of the bathrooms contains all this strange makeshift plumbing. Finally, the whole place was wired with a state-of-the-art security system. I had to hire a security expert to explain everything to me."

Gayle said, "All those features seem consistent with a photography lab except maybe the security system. Is it a high crime area?"

Sanders scowled. "I don't think I would classify it as a crime ridden area."

"What kind of businesses are in the neighborhood?"

"Car repair, manufacturing, and a small mom-and-pop brewery."

Gayle's eyes widened. "There's a mom-and-pop brewery? You can walk down and get a beer after a long day of painting."

Sanders laughed. "That's true."

"Did you have to make very many changes to the layout of the building?"

Sanders nodded. "With a few minor changes, I transformed it into a nice studio and exhibition space."

"That sounds exciting Sanders. I'll have to come visit soon."

"I'm counting on it, Gayle."

Gayle said, "Let's get back to you. What are you going to do to address your reclusive concern?"

Sanders took a drink of his wine. Before he could answer, the waiter brought dinner. Their conversation drifted in a different direction until they were waiting for the check to arrive. Gayle said, "You never answered my question on what you're going to do about your lack of social interaction."

Sanders grimaced. "I just joined a dating site this afternoon."

"Really? What site did you select?"

"Nonpareil Match."

Gayle furrowed her eyebrows. "I've never heard of Nonpareil."

"Until I did some research, I never heard of it either. All the major sites had comparable ratings.

To be honest, I choose Nonpareil because I liked the name."

Gayle rolled her eyes. "That's certainly not overwhelming evidence that Nonpareil is the best."

Sanders said, "I agree. Nonetheless, I spent this afternoon researching sites and setting up an account."

"Some of my friends say that they never would've found a significant other if not for the internet."

"Did these friends of yours ever have any horrible experiences?"

Gayle laughed. "Well, if they did, no one fessed up to it. Although, I did see a news article the other day on the internet about a woman who met a guy on some dating website, and he ended up being a convicted felon. This guy seemed perfectly charming until the woman discovered he had emptied her life savings out of her investment accounts."

Sanders finished off the last swig of his wine. "That's a little discouraging. I promise I'll be forthcoming if I have a bad experience."

Gayle said, "Let's agree to meet again for dinner in a few months and you can apprise me of all your romantic encounters."

"You're making some pretty bold assumptions that any woman would agree to meet me."

"A retired attorney and successful artist. You'll be a chick magnet."

Sanders laughed. "More like an over the hill chick magnet."

The waiter arrived with the check and placed it in the middle of the table. Both Sanders and Gayle reached for it.

Gayle patted his hand. She said, "Not a chance in hell that birthday boy is getting the check."

Sanders smiled. "Thank you, Gayle. I invited you to dinner and fully intended to pay the check."

"You always pay the check Sanders. I'll make you a deal. You pay for dinner when we reconvene to discuss the progress you've made in your social life, and I'll get it tonight."

"You win. Thank you again. It was a fun evening."

Sanders waited for his car at the valet stand and watched as Gayle drove away. He felt contented after a wonderful dinner shared with an old friend. But Gayle's story about the woman meeting a convicted felon on a dating website was sobering.

What if I have the same experience as that poor woman?

Chapter 2

Sanders woke up early and decided to get in some exercise before breakfast. He put on his runners and took the elevator down to the lobby. It was a warm September morning. He walked the short distance over to Klyde Warren Park, a narrow green five acres resting on top of Woodall Rogers Freeway. Sanders like how it tied the trendy Uptown area to downtown Dallas. Since it was completed in 2012, Klyde Warren Park has been a popular destination for Dallas residents, especially on the weekends. Another reason he liked it.

Sanders forgot it was Saturday until he reached the park and spotted people practicing group yoga. Seeing all the activity was energizing. At a brisk pace, he walked the perimeter of the park twice. Every time Sanders passed a single woman near his age, he wondered if she might be on the Nonpareil Match website. By the end of his second lap, he had speculated enough about the dating habits of the opposite sex and headed back to his apartment.

It was early afternoon and Sanders had procrastinated long enough completing his profile on Nonpareil. Now was the time to exert a little discipline and get to work.

Where to begin?

Sanders uploaded a couple of recent pictures of

himself. He selected them over the others because they were closer to depicting his age but also concealed some of his wrinkles.

Will any woman ever get past my pictures, or will they see them and immediately be scared off?

Sanders considered not including pictures, but the site administrators strongly advised against it. Now was time to complete the Interests section. He listed painting, visiting art museums and galleries, modern dance, fine dining, travel, wine, and reading. These were truly his interests, but he thought they also projected an air of refinement.

He completed the Education section, listing his undergraduate degree, law degree and at the end, his wine sommelier certification he had received a few years ago. The next section was Politics. He chuckled to himself and said out loud, "This will definitely be a significant filter."

While Dallas County had been trending blue for several years, it was evenly divided between conservatives and liberals. The Dallas suburbs were overwhelming conservative. Sanders was honest but decided to take the safest course available. He described himself as socially liberal and fiscally prudent, reasoning that the description would most likely cause some confusion, however it was accurate.

The next section was Favorite Books. His first choice was a no brainer. He loved Jack Kerouac's *On the Road*. It was his all-time favorite book. The section called for three books. One of Sanders' undergraduate majors was philosophy. Thomas Hobbes' *Leviathan* caught Sander's attention. Sanders was impressed with Hobbes description of the state of human nature as a "war of all against all". As an undergraduate, Sanders had considered this perspective to be overly cynical. Nonetheless as he grew older, Sanders concluded that Hobbes nailed it.

For his third book, Sanders needed to be creative. He decided to go with a book he enjoyed as a young boy. Listing a children's book may raise some eyebrows but it also may generate some curiosity. Sanders listed Dr. Seuss' *The Cat in the Hat*. How could he go wrong with Dr. Seuss?

The remaining section was Targeted Age Range. Sanders opted to go with a minimum of forty years old with no maximum age. The section could always be modified if he changed his mind. He clicked the "save" button and breathed a heavy sigh. He was done.

Sanders checked the time. It was now already 4:30 p.m. Too late to drive over to his artist studio. Instead, he poured himself a glass of chardonnay and went out on his porch. His twelfth story apartment offered a stunning view of downtown Dallas in the background and Klyde Warren Park in the foreground.

I wonder if my profile will get any hits.

Chapter 3

On Monday afternoon, Sanders parked his Fiat Spider in one of the five places in front of the building that housed his studio and gallery. He unlocked the front door, relocked it, and disarmed the security system. Sanders selected a station on Pandora and in an instant music flooded the entire building. Wiring the entire building for sound had been no small investment but well worth it.

Sanders got settled in for a full afternoon of painting. As he was ready to squeeze some paint onto a palatte, his cell phone chimed, indicating that one of the outside motion detectors had been triggered. He walked out of his studio through the main part of the building towards the front door. From the front windows, a man's face was pressed against the glass, as he attempted to peer through the dark tinted windows.

Sanders retreated to his office, which housed his security monitors and intercom. Through the intercom Sanders said, "Hello, may I help you with something?"

The man took a step backwards and stared up at intercom speaker mounted under the eaves of the building. He said, "Hey, man, I need to talk to Reggie."

Sanders sighed. "There's no one by that name

here. Are you sure you have the right place?"

The man scowled at the monitor. "You don't understand man, I need to talk to Reggie really bad!"

Sanders suspected maybe the man was seeking one of the prior tenants who were photographers. He said, "Was Reggie a photographer?"

The man frowned, "Was he a what? Why are you messing with me? Who the hell are you anyway?"

Sanders shot back, "I'm the owner of this building. The prior owner told me some photographers leased this space before I purchased it. That's why I asked you if maybe this Reggie was a photographer."

The man paced and slammed his right fist into his left palm. He shouted, "Damn it. Let me in!"

In a voice as calm as he could make, Sanders said, "Sir, I don't know you and I'm not inclined to let you in."

The man walked out of view of the security camera. Sanders stared at the monitor a few more minutes to make certain the guy was gone. His phone chimed again. The motion detector at the rear door was tripped. Sanders watched on the monitor as the man attempted to open the metal back door.

Sanders whispered to himself, "You're not getting in that door unless you brought a battering ram."

The man stood by the back door and stared down at his phone. He appeared to be texting someone. A few more minutes passed before the man vanished from the monitor.

Sander stood up. *After all this excitement, I think*

I'll do a little painting.

He painted the remainder of the afternoon until 5:00 p.m. when he cleaned his brushes and neatened his art table. Time for a well-deserved glass of wine. Sanders opened his refrigerator and extracted a bottle of chardonnay and poured a glass. He plopped down on the sofa in his studio and pulled out his phone to check emails. An alert from Nonpareil Match indicated Sanders had received a message in his inbox. He thought it was probably nothing and opted to wait until he got home before checking it.

Sanders armed the security alarm and exited his studio. His mood lightened when the man who had appeared at his door earlier was nowhere in sight. The goal on the way home was to avoid rush hour traffic. Sanders took the back streets back to his apartment. After dinner, he got on his laptop and pulled up the Nonpareil website.

There were two messages in his inbox. Both were general inquiries from two different women inviting Sanders to check out their profiles. The first profile was from a young woman seeking a sugar daddy.

At least she's honest about her intentions.

Without hesitation, he deleted it before reading any further. The second was from a woman in her late forties. Her online name was Z Kat. Sanders read her profile and did not see any immediate deal breakers. She was a hospice caregiver.

Sanders was always intrigued with those who chose hospice care as a profession. He knew from his legal background in health benefits that hospice was a type of health care that focused on the palliation of terminally ill patient's pain and symptoms while attending to their emotional and spiritual needs at the end of life. Patients in hospice care were those not expected to live beyond six months at most. He surmised it would be a challenging profession for one to choose.

Kat included the maximum three pictures. From her pictures, she appeared to be a tall thin woman with strawberry blond hair. In one of her pictures, Kat was photographed wearing scrubs.

Sanders decided to send a message to Z Kat:

> Hello Kat,
> Thank you for reaching out to me. Truthfully, I find this whole process a little awkward. However, I enjoyed reading your profile. Very impressed to learn that you are a hospice caregiver. What a wonderful and, I would assume, very challenging profession to choose. In addition, your pictures are quite lovely. If you're interested, I would like to exchange messages to see if we might have similar interests.

Sanders paused typing and decided to keep the initial message short.

Hell, she probably won't even reply after seeing my pictures!

He hit send and decided he had enough of Nonpareil Match for one day.

Chapter 4

Sanders woke up and grabbed his iPad off the nightstand. As was his custom, he began the day by checking his email. In it was an email from Nonpareil Match indicating he had a new message. Sanders accessed the Nonpareil Match website, entered his username and password. Three new messages were in his mailbox. Two were standard contacts from women inviting him to check out their profiles.

The third message was a response from Kat. Sanders open the message and read:

> Why are you asking me that?
> Is it because my name is Kat?
> I know it is not wet but sunny.
> But we can have lots of good times that is funny!
> Kat

Sanders was bewildered.

What the hell does that mean? Is this some kind of riddle or is she a flake, or both?

He set his iPad down and decided he needed some fresh air. Sanders put on his sweats and runners, and then headed to the Katy Trail for some exercise. As he was walking, he could not get Kat's message out of his head. In a strange sort of way, it sounded familiar. *But where?* Three miles into his walk, it occurred to Sanders that the rhyming of the message resembled Dr. Seuss.

She must have sent this type of message because he listed in his profile *The Cat in the Hat* as one of his favorite books. As soon as he got back to his apartment, Sanders search the internet for *The Cat in the Hat.* To his surprise someone had posted a PDF containing a complete illustrated version of it and *The Cat in the Hat Comes Back.*

He went back and reread Kat's message and then started reading *The Cat in the Hat.* On page 6. was a slightly different version of a paragraph than the one Kat had included in her message. But there could be no mistake that she plagiarized the text from Dr. Seuss.

Actually, that's pretty clever for an initial message to send. It demonstrates in a humorous way that Kat has read my profile and that she's also very creative.

Sanders accessed his account on Nonpareil and went to his mailbox. He typed a message to her.

> Hi Kat, thank you for responding to my message. I must admit I was baffled by your email for several hours before it occurred to me that you were emulating Dr. Seuss. What an ingenious way to respond. I am afraid I am not that imaginative. Sanders

He again thought a very brief message was appropriate. If Kat responded by showing some interest, then a lengthy one creating a dialogue would be in order.

Sanders lunched at Savor. Sanders enjoyed eating at the bar where he could watch through the window the crowd of people enjoying the park's amenities. After lunch, he slow-trotted the short distance back to his apartment. Sanders checked his watch for the time. If he hurried, he could get several hours of painting done at his studio before the start of rush hour traffic.

Traffic was mild in route to the Core District. The usual used cars were parallel parked on each side of Interurban Street where his studio was located. Every time Sanders drove on Interurban Street, he speculated as to why all these small used car dealerships had clustered so close together on one street. Would it not have been better to find a location where you had little to no competition.

As he pulled his Spider up to his building, he noticed an envelope was attached to the front door. Sanders removed the enveloped, unlocked the door, and disengaged the security alarm. He stared at the sealed envelope.

It's probably some kind of advertisement. I'll open it later.

Sanders tossed the envelope on the desk in his office and headed to his studio and switched the lights on. It was 2:45 p.m., which gave him several hours to paint until rush hour traffic began.

A large half-finished abstract landscape painting rested on the easel. Sanders stared at it for several minutes before deciding his course of action. He squeezed several different color paints onto a palette and mixed them together along with some medium. The next two hours were spent adding detail to a small portion of the painting.

Satisfied with the day's progress, Sanders cleaned his brushes and retreated to his office. He plopped down into his office chair and retrieved a letter opener in his top desk drawer. Sanders took care as he opened the envelope. Inside was a single page of typewritten words:

> Immediate action is required! All the funds have been deposited as agreed. Any further delay beyond one week from today will be considered a breach. Damages will be pursued.

Sanders read the text several times in the attempt to glean meaning.

What the hell is this all about? Is this note somehow connected to the man who tried to get in the building the last time I was here?

Sanders leaned back in his chair and checked his phone for emails. Nothing grabbed his interest. He anticipated he might have received a response from Kat. But no such luck. Before exiting his office,

Sanders glanced at the exterior security cameras on the monitor. No one was in sight. He set the security alarm and locked the door to his building.

Traffic was light as he drove to his apartment near downtown Dallas. During his drive, he kept thinking about the note left on his front door. The language of the text sounded almost contractual in nature. He pondered what was meant by "Damages will be pursued."

SANDERS SPENT THE BETTER part of the evening watching the 1973 film, *The Mackintosh Man*, starring Paul Newman. He was feeling nostalgic about his youth. Watching movies made in the 1970s somehow provided a bit of comfort. He decided to check his emails one last time before heading to bed. Sure enough, he spotted an email from Z Kat and opened it.

> You aced it, Sanders! I wasn't certain you would decipher my Kat speak.
> Congratulations! Yes, let's get acquainted. Would you care to meet somewhere soon for a glass of wine? After all, it is fun to have fun. But you have to know how. Thoughts?

Sanders scratched his head.

So much for exchanging emails to see if we have similar interests. Hell, she just jumped right in and proposed an in-person meeting. What did she mean by "After all, it is fun to have fun. But you have to know how"? *Is that another Dr. Seuss reference?*

Sanders grabbed his iPad off the nightstand and opened the PDF of *The Cat in the Hat* he had saved from earlier. He scrolled through a few pages until he found verbatim the language Kat had lifted from the book.

He grimaced. *One time referencing Dr. Seuss is charming. A second time...*

Sanders stared at her message for several minutes until he decided to sleep on it. He set his iPad down on the nightstand and crawled under the covers in his bed. Aided by effects of the cocktail he had consumed while watching the movie, he drifted off to sleep.

Chapter 5

It was cool crisp October Saturday morning. He decided he needed some fresh air and leisurely strolled over to Klyde Warren Park.

Sanders had forgotten it was the weekend. All his days seemed to blur together. The urban park was vibrant with activity. He found an empty bench and sat down to take it all in. Young families were out in droves.

Sanders smiled as he watched as a dad was demonstrating to his young son how to throw a football. He was flooded with memories of his childhood which lifted his spirits. Sanders pulled out his iPhone and checked his email. He reread the email he had received last night from Kat. Before he could talk himself out of it, he typed a brief response.

> Hi Kat, it was nice to hear back from you. Your suggestion of meeting for a glass of wine is stellar. Did you have a specific place in mind for us to meet? I hope you are enjoying this beautiful Saturday morning. I am typing this message while sitting on a bench in Klyde Warren Park. If you have never visited the park on a Saturday morning, it is a popular place to be when the weather is nice. I live nearby so I often frequent it.
> Happy Saturday!
> Sanders

Short and to the point is probably the best approach.

Sanders rose from the park bench and ambled the short distance back to his apartment building. As he waited for the elevator in the lobby, he checked emails. Kat had already responded. Before he could open the email, the elevator doors slid apart. Sanders pocketed his phone, stepped inside, and rode to the twelfth floor where his apartment was located. He walked through the door and plopped down on his living room couch.

Might as well check to see what Kat has to say.

Sanders opened Kat's email.

> I have my afternoon free tomorrow, so why don't we meet at 4:00 p.m. for a glass of wine at Savor. I assume that works for you since you live close by. Besides, it might rain. I adore a gray rainy day, don't you?
> Kat

Sanders walked out on his balcony overlooking downtown Dallas. Savor was a convenient choice, for sure. He wondered, though, about the part of her email where she confessed to 'adoring a rainy day'. Was that another Dr. Seuss reference? Sanders reached for his iPad and logged into his Nonpareil Match account. He checked his messages and discovered he had been contacted by three potential matches. Sanders ignored the messages and after a couple of clicks he pulled up Kat's profile.

He realized that after she first contacted him, he had not checked out her whole profile. Her list of favorite books consisted of one book, *In Cold Blood* by Truman Capote. He had read the book one summer while in college. It details the true story of the murders of four members of a family in rural Kansas.

Why on earth would someone list that book as their favorite on a dating website? Whom are they trying to attract?

Sanders scrolled to Kat's music preferences. She listed the alternative rock group Garbage instead of a genre and Handel.

That's an interesting combination. I wonder what she finds so special about Garbage? Why list only one band and a classical composer instead of a genre? This may be one huge mistake, but I am going to meet this Kat.

Sanders sent an email confirming the date, rain or shine.

Chapter 6

Sanders spent his Sunday morning walking the Katy Trail. The trail was once an abandoned railroad track that ran from the west end of downtown Dallas north through Dallas. The city of Dallas converted the trail into a hike and bike trail in the late 1990s. Part of the trail bordered one of Dallas' earliest parks, Reverchon Park. Sanders devoted several days a week to walking the trail or exploring the paths in the park alongside Turtle Creek.

During his walk, he vacillated between pondering how the conversation with Kat would go and what he should wear. While Sanders felt clueless about the potential conversation, he thought he could nail the wardrobe issue. He elected to wear a light blue dress shirt, charcoal gray sport coat and blue jeans.

At 3:50 p.m., on a misty overcast cool afternoon, Sanders exited his apartment building and walked the short distance around the block to Savor. He arrived five minutes later.

The restaurant was almost deserted. It was Sunday afternoon and too late for lunch and too early for the happy hour crowd. Sanders opened the door and right away headed to the left side of the bar. From that vantage point, he could watch all the activity in Klyde Warren Park while keeping an eye on the front door. He would not have any difficulty recognizing

Kat, assuming the pictures from Nonpareil Match were accurate.

At 4:10 p.m., a beige SUV pulled up to the valet stand. Sanders watched as a tall strawberry blonde stepped out of the SUV. She was dressed in a navy pantsuit and white blouse. After the valet handed her a slip of paper, they walked over to the front door. He opened the door for her, and she flashed a killer smile.

Sanders sat without moving as the woman's eyes scanned the interior of the restaurant. They made eye contact and Sanders stood up behind his stool as she made her way over to him.

The woman spoke first. "I presume you're Sanders."

He smiled. "I'm definitely Sanders, and you must be Kat."

The two of them hugged for a moment. Sanders felt her hand slip something into his shirt pocket. He raised his eyebrows.

Kat said, "Oh, I startled you. Sanders, you don't mind safeguarding my valet ticket, do you?"

Sanders glanced down at his shirt pocket. "Of course."

He motioned toward the barstool next to where he sat. "Would you like to sit at the bar or get a table?"

Kat scanned the crowd at the restaurant. "The bar is perfect. Besides, you're all settled in here."

She slid onto the stool next to him. The bartender was hand washing some glasses and did not notice

Kat. She said, "What are you drinking, Sanders?"

He looked down at his wine glass. "I'm having a Hess Chardonnay."

Kat flipped her hair. "How is it?"

He grinned. "Not bad. I think it's the best chardonnay they serve by the glass."

The bartender overheard their conversation and approached them. "May I get you something to drink?"

Kat leaned forward. "I'll have what the gentleman is drinking."

They both watched as the bartender poured Kat a glass of wine.

Sanders broke the silence. "So happy you suggested we meet here. It's always fun to watch all the action in park."

The bartender set her glass of wine in front of her. She smiled at him. "Thank you."

"My pleasure."

Kat turned to Sanders and extended her wine glass toward him. "Salute."

He picked his glass up and clinked it against hers. "Cheers."

They both took a swig of wine.

Kat said, "So, I believe you said in one of your emails that you live nearby."

Sanders gestured with his glass in the direction of his apartment. "I live in a high rise building a block from here."

"That's convenient."

"Yes, I've enjoyed living so close to the Arts District. How about you, where do you live?"

Kat took a drink of her wine. "Near Coit and Campbell in North Dallas."

"Nice area."

She nodded and pointed outside as light rain spattered the sidewalk. Kat said, "What a beautiful day."

Sanders furrowed his brow. "I suppose so, if you like rainy days. It certainly cleared out the park."

She batted her eyes. "The sun did not shine. It was too wet to play. So, we sat in the house all that cold, cold, wet day."

Sanders was bewildered. "Excuse me."

Kat smiled at him. "It's from one of your favorite books."

He grimaced and then perked up. "Of course, it's the opening sentence of *The Cat in the Hat*."

"Bingo." Kat laughed out loud.

Sanders took a swig of his wine. "I wondered earlier today where our conversation would lead. I never dreamt we would be discussing *The Cat in the Hat*."

Kat reached over and patted Sanders's hand. "What would you like to talk about?"

He leaned forward, resting both hands on the bar. "Tell me about your work in hospice care."

Kat's demeanor changed, at once very severe. "First of all, do you understand what it means to be in hospice?"

"Yes, I'm familiar with Health Benefits. I specialized in that area of the law for more time than I care to remember."

Kat picked up here wine glass but did not take a drink. She stared at the wine in her glass. After a pause she said, "Then you understand that my clients are terminally ill and are typically not expected to live more than six months. I give them physical and emotional care to make their final days as tolerable as possible."

Sanders leaned toward her. "I would imagine you get very attached to your clients."

"Very close. It breaks my heart every time I lose one. I know the end is inevitable but that doesn't make it any easier."

Sanders wanted to lighten the conversation. "Well your work is very admirable and appreciated."

Kat sighed. "Thank you. It's not for everyone. Tell me about yourself. I already know that you like Dr. Seuss."

Sanders laughed. "What else is there to know?"

She tapped his arm in a playful gesture. "So, tell me about your decision to transition from practicing law to art. Something more than what was in your profile on Nonpareil. You don't just stop doing something you've successfully done for twenty plus years and suddenly decide one day you're going to do something else."

It was Sanders turn to look severe. He swallowed before speaking. "I represented health insurance companies who were sued by their insureds over benefits denied under their policies. Often the decisions made in the trial determined whether the insureds would be covered for some expensive treatment."

Sanders paused to take a drink of wine. "Some of these people had to forego medical treatments simply because they couldn't afford them. I grew weary of practicing this type of law, so I retired."

Kat studied his face. "You pretty damn good looking when you're somber."

Sanders shook his head. "You can't be serious. Is that some reference to Dr. Seuss that I'm missing?"

Kat smiled, "No, I'm dead serious. I wouldn't be sitting here if I didn't think you were handsome." Her cell phone chimed. She opened her purse and pulled out her phone.

Sanders studied her expression as she read a text message. "Bad news?"

Kat sighed. "It's the other caregiver for my client, Glenda Davidson. Apparently, she has taken a turn for the worse. It looks like it might be a difficult night."

"I'm sorry."

Kat finished off her wine with one huge swig. "I apologize, Sanders, but I'm going to have to leave so I can get to work early."

"No need to apologize. I understand completely."

She stood up and Sanders followed suite. Sanders paid the bill and they both exited Savor. When they neared the valet stand, Kat turned toward Sanders and gave him a quick kiss on his cheek. "Thank you for understanding."

"Of course. He fished for the valet ticket that Kat had slipped into his shirt pocket and handed it to the valet."

When the valet returned with Kat's SUV, Sanders handed him a ten dollar bill. Before sliding into her car, Kat smiled at him. "I enjoyed our brief visit."

He took a step towards her car. "Me, too. Be safe."

She nodded and eased her car away from the curb. Sanders caught a glimpse of her rear license plate which read LUNA-WLF.

What does Luna wlf mean?

Sanders fished his cell phone out of his coat pocket and pulled up the Safari browser. He typed in the word Luna Wlf on a search engine. The closet match was Luna Wolf which refers to the alpha female in a wolf pack.

Well, that's certainly interesting! I wonder if that's a vanity license plate or a pure coincidence.

As he walked the short distance back to his apartment building, Sanders wondered if Kat really had to leave early or if she used the text she received as an excuse to leave.

Chapter 7

On Monday morning, Sanders slept in late. He spent the better part of the night having one of his recurring nightmares where he was trying an impossible lawsuit before an unsympathetic judge.

As he gained consciousness, he heaved a sigh of relief that the nightmare was over and that he was retired from practicing law. He debated whether to get some exercise but decided against it.

After an early lunch, Sanders was eager to get to his studio. He arrived at the small parking lot in front of his building. As usual, Interurban Street was lined with various cars from the surrounding used car lots bearing For Sale signs on their dashboards.

Sanders unlocked his front door and switched off the security alarm just inside the building. He walked through the gallery part of the building to the room on the front right side which housed his studio. After plopping down in his studio chair, Sanders went through his customary practice of staring at his unfinished painting plotting his next move.

As he was reaching for a tube of paint, he jumped at the sound of his exterior doorknob jiggling. Sanders twirled around in his chair in the direction of the door but could not see anyone through the narrow heavily tinted window panel next to the door.

He retreated to his office so he could check the monitors in his office for the outside security cameras. The only thing in sight from either camera was his FIAT Spider parked in front.

I wonder who that was? Maybe it was the mailman or someone attempting to make a delivery.

Sanders returned to his studio and spent several hours painting. When he glanced up at his wall clock, it was almost 4:30 p.m. Satisfied with his work for the afternoon, Sanders decided to head back to his apartment. He cleaned his brushes and neatened up his studio and returned to the other side of the gallery.

Sanders set the alarm and locked the door behind him. He took one step toward his car and reversed course to check his mailbox for any mail. Sanders retrieved two envelopes of mail and studied them briefly to determine if they were of consequence. When he looked up, two men were standing next to his Spider. Both were dressed in blue jeans, casual shirts, and sport coats.

Of the two, the heaviest sported sunglasses. He said in a gruff voice, "You own this building?"

Sanders said, "May I ask who you are?"

The man with sunglasses approached Sanders. "Trust me, the less you know about us, the better off you are. Understand?"

"To answer... your question. Yes, I... I own this building."

The other man took several steps until he was next

to the man with sunglasses. Both men were now only a few feet from Sanders. The man with sunglasses opened his sport coat just enough to reveal a holster and pistol. "How long have you owned this building?"

"Just a little while. I purchased it back in September."

The man without glasses spoke for the first time. "Was it occupied when you acquired it?"

The palms of his hands turned clammy as they always did when he was under duress. "No, the prior owner told me he used to lease it to some photographers. But they broke the lease and vanished."

The man with the sunglasses said, "Did these photographers leave anything behind when they vanished, as you say?"

Sanders shook his head. "No, it was deserted when I took possession."

The other man said, "What do you use the building for now?"

"I'm an artist. I have my studio and gallery here."

The man with the sunglasses growled, "Care to show us?"

Sanders swallowed. "I assume I don't have a choice."

The man with sunglasses said, "That's very perceptive of you."

Sanders dug his right hand into his pocket for his keys and both men rushed toward him. The man without glasses grabbed Sanders right arm before he could pull it out of his pocket. He growled, "Take your hand out of your pocket slowly. There better be nothing but keys in your hand."

Sanders pulled his keys out and almost dropped them. He unlocked the door to his building but before opening the door, he said, "I have switch off the security alarm as soon as we enter."

Neither of the two men responded. They waited behind Sanders as he entered the code to disarm the security alarm.

The man with sunglasses flipped the light switches next to the door, until all the track lighting blazed throughout building. "What's in that bar area over there?"

"I keep my wine and other items I plan on using when I have an event in the gallery."

The other man said, "I'll check it out."

Sanders and the man with sunglasses followed the other man over to the bar and watched as he pulled out every drawer and examined the contents. He even checked inside the small refrigerator nestled behind the bar. "It's clean."

Sanders said, "May I ask just exactly what it is you're looking for?"

The man with sunglasses shrugged. "Ask away. But as I said earlier, the less you know the better off you are."

"Okay, don't tell me then."

The men went through the room that Sanders used as his office with a fine-tooth comb. Sanders was relieved he had not yet brought any of his personal files to his office. The man without sunglasses made his way through the office, often stopping to tap on the interior walls with the palm of his hand.

The next room was a small bathroom adjacent to the office. The man with sunglasses went into it alone. Sanders listened as the man pulled out the two drawers and opened the vanity cabinet. He exited the bathroom and said, "Nothing."

The man with glasses said, "Let's check that room out." He pointed in the direction of the room Sanders used as his studio.

All three men walked inside the studio. The man without sunglasses checked under the cushions on the sofa and chairs. He opened the container where Sanders stored his paints and ran his hand through them.

The man with sunglasses said, "What's in back?"

Sanders said, "Around the corner is a broom closet and another restroom."

The man with sunglasses barked, "Go check out both rooms."

The small closet contained a broom, mop, and some empty boxes. The restroom was identical in size to the first bathroom. The only difference was the shape of the mirror over the vanity and some unusual plumbing.

The man without glasses searched the closet and restroom. He returned with a frown. "Not a damn thing."

They walked back into the gallery area of the

building. The man with glasses said, "Any other rooms?"

Sanders shook his head. "No, you've seen everything."

The man with sunglasses grunted. "There's no drop-down panels where they could have hidden it?" He pointed up to ceiling of the old building.

The only thing on the ceiling was air condition and heating ductwork that had been painted black. The man without glasses scanned the room before he said, "Do you have a ladder?"

Sanders nodded. "There's one leaning against the wall by my paintings near the back door."

The man with sunglasses and Sanders watched as the other man walked around the building . He stopped every few yards and climbed up the ladder to check the seams in the ductwork. The man climbed down one final time. "It's clean."

The man with the sunglasses said, "They must have taken it with them. Let's get out of here." He motioned with his head in the direction of the front door and said to Sanders, "After you."

Sanders felt weak-kneed as he stumbled in the direction of the front door. He wondered what was going to happen. When they reached the front door, Sanders paused. "Are we exiting the building?"

The man with the sunglasses snapped, "Just open the damn door."

Sanders opened the door and felt a hand on his shoulder. The man with sunglasses said, "Lock the door, face the wall, and wait ten minutes after we leave before you move an inch. You got that?"

Sanders nodded, "Yes, I understand." He locked the door and faced the wall as instructed.

The man with sunglasses said, "Oh and one more thing. I wouldn't advise telling anyone we were here."

Without moving Sanders said, "I have no reason to tell a soul."

The man with sunglasses said, "Correct answer."

Sanders strained to listen as the sound of men's footsteps on pavement faded when they rounded the corner of the building. He tapped his foot while he waited for what he thought was at least ten minutes before he looked around. No one was in sight.

He hurried over to his Spider. Before he unlocked the car door, he swiveled his head around at the sound of a truck driving by. It appeared to be a delivery truck of some sort. Relieved, Sanders unlocked his car and slid into the driver's seat. He exhaled and started the engine.

My God, what was that all about? What the hell were they looking for?

Chapter 8

By early Wednesday afternoon, three days had passed since Sanders's date with Kat. He had made no effort to contact her, nor had she reached out to him. Sanders decided to send her a brief message before he headed to his studio for what he hoped would be an uneventful day of painting.

> Hi Kat,
> How are you doing. I hope is well. You immediately came to mind today when it began to rain. As I recall, you told me that you are only happy when it rains.

Sanders had not returned to his studio since Monday when he was confronted by the two mysterious men. He turned off Arapaho Drive onto Interurban Street as he had every time he had driven to his studio since he purchased the building.

As Sanders pulled into the parking lot in front, he remembered he had not set the security alarm when he left Monday. The experience with the two men had rattled him and all he wanted to do that afternoon was to get out of there as quickly as possible. He parked in the middle space of his small lot, as was his custom.

God, I hope no one has broken in.

Sanders unlocked the door, switched on all the lights, and relocked the door behind him. He hurried through each of the rooms in the small building. Everything was as he had left it. A quick inspection of the rear door revealed it was locked, too.

Breathing a sigh of relief, Sanders went into his studio and plopped down on the sofa. He opened his iPad and checked his email. Nothing of interest popped up. He logged into his Nonpareil Match account. No response from Kat.

Instead of beginning the afternoon painting, Sanders decided he needed to do something to boost his spirits. The first order of business was to switch on some music to fill the entire building. Satisfied with the ambiance it created, he curated the walls of the gallery for the first time with his art that he had taken such care to store in the back. Dressing up the white empty walls enhanced the whole dramatic appearance of the gallery space. Sanders pondered why he had waited so long to do it. He climbed up on his latter to adjust the lighting on a few paintings. When he finished, he stepped off the bottom rung, stood back, and smiled up at the artwork.

The space looks like a proper art gallery now.

The sign bearing the name Sanders had chosen for his building was scheduled to be installed the next day. He had struggled with determining the appropriate name.

While painting one afternoon, Sanders had a sudden epiphany. The name that came to him was Interurban Contemporary. It had a certain edgy urbane quality. The name would stand out among all the neighboring used car dealerships and repair shops.

By 4:30 p.m., Sanders decided to call it a day and head back to his apartment. He checked the security monitors in his office to make sure no unwelcome guests were waiting outside for him.

God, I hope those guys don't come back!

Chapter 9

The next morning, Sanders retrieved the *Dallas Morning News* from outside his apartment door. Armed with a cup of coffee, he was ready to spend the next thirty minutes reading yesterday's news. Sanders perused the Sports Section before launching into the local news in the Metropolitan Section. He flipped through the Obituaries which followed the local headlines. Scanning the names listed, Sanders stopped at the obituary titled Glenda Davidson.

Why does that name seem familiar?

He read the brief obituary and grimaced. Nothing in the obituary triggered any kind of memory of why her name resonated with him. He gasped when he remembered Kat had mentioned her client was named Mrs. Davidson.

Was this Kat's client?

Sanders re-read the obituary. Glenda Davidson resided on Straight Lane in Dallas and was active in Preston Hollow Presbyterian Church. The church family comforted Mrs. Davidson in her final days. The obituary noted she was survived solely by a niece who resided in Frankfurt, Germany. The last sentence stated the family requests that donations be made to the Alzheimer's Foundation of America in lieu of flowers.

SANDERS GLANCED UP at the clock on his studio wall. It was 3:00 p.m. The sound of metal clanging against brick drowned out for a moment the ambient music inside the building. Sanders scrambled out of his studio to the front of the gallery space. Through the dark tinted windows, he could just make out the shadow of two ladders leaning against the front of his building. Sanders opened the door and peered outside. Two men were unloading his sign from the bed of a truck parked next to the FIAT Spider.

Sanders shouted from the doorway, "You guys need any help?"

One of the men said, "No, we can manage. Thanks anyway."

Sanders watched as the men climbed the ladders, each holding an end of the sign. He walked out to the edge of the parking lot to get a better look as the men began installing his sign. Before the men were finished, several cars slowed down on Interurban Street. They seemed curious to see what the men were installing. Sanders smiled.

Most folks around here will be surprised or befuddled by a sign that reads Interurban Contemporary. They probably assumed it was a fancy name for a used car dealership or repair shop.

When the men were finished, one of them had Sanders sign the invoice to acknowledge receipt and successful installation of the sign. He went back into his building and headed to the refrigerator behind his gallery bar.

Time for a celebratory glass of chardonnay!

Sanders walked around the interior of the gallery space, admiring the art he had hung the previous day. Three knocks on the front door interrupted his self-guided tour. Sanders furrowed his brow. He wondered if the men who had just installed the sign had returned for some reason. Sanders cracked open the door.

Much to his surprise a young woman he guessed to be in her mid-thirties stood outside. She wore sunglasses and was dressed in faded blue jeans and a white blouse. Her blond hair was pulled back into a ponytail.

Sanders said, "Can I help you with something?"

The woman removed her sunglasses. "What is this place, anyway?"

He squinted, trying to decipher how to answer the question. "Well, it's a new art gallery."

The woman shook her head in the direction of the new sign overhead. "I drive down Interurban almost every day and I don't remember ever seeing the sign before."

Sanders smiled. "That's because it was just installed today. Would you care to come in look around?"

"Sure." She walked toward Sanders and extended her hand. "I'm Sara."

He shook her hand. "Pleased to meet you. I'm Sanders."

Sara walked into the gallery and Sanders closed the door behind her. "Is this your gallery?" she said.

Sanders nodded. "Yes, I bought the building a few months ago. I really haven't had it open to the public." He paused. "I guess until today."

"I love art," she said. "I always thought I was going to major in art in college, but my parents insisted that I do something more practical." She rolled her eyes. "So, I got a business degree."

Sanders spotted his wine glass resting on the bar. "Listen, I just poured myself a glass of chardonnay. Would you care for a glass of wine?"

Sara's eyes lit up. "I'd love a glass of chardonnay."

Sanders motioned toward the bar, and she followed him over to it. Sara plopped down on one the bar stools and laid her purse on top of the bar. He pulled a bottle out of his refrigerator and held the label up for Sara to see.

She squinted as she read it. "Ramey Chardonnay. I'm impressed."

Sanders smiled. "Drinking excellent wine is my Achilles heel."

Sara laughed. "That's a good Achilles heel to have."

After he poured her a glass, he gestured toward the gallery. "Care to have a look at the art?"

She slid off the barstool right away. "I'd love to see your art."

They spent almost a half of hour walking around the perimeter of the gallery, discussing the art.

Sanders then showed Sara his artist studio.

"So, this is where all the magic happens," Sara said in a playful tone.

He smiled. "Well, this is where I paint anyway."

A cell phone chimed from inside her jeans pocket. She retrieved it, stared at the screen, and grimaced. "I'm going to have to run."

"A problem at work?"

She frowned. "Something like that. Do you mind if I use your restroom before I go?"

"Of course not."

"I just need to get my purse."

She exited the studio and hurried in the direction of the bar. Sanders followed her and stopped in the middle of the gallery. He waited for her to collect her purse before he spoke.

"Let me show you where it's located."

She briskly walked past him and feign a smile. "No worries. I think I noticed earlier."

Sanders's eyebrows shot up. "Okay."

How did she notice the bathroom earlier? There is no signage, and we were nowhere near it.

He watched as she made her way through the gallery and disappeared around the corner where the small storage closet and bathroom were located. Sanders was grateful Sara chose to use the bathroom he intended to reserve for guests and not the one he deemed his own, which was accessed through his office.

Sanders walked over to the bar and slid onto one

of the barstools. He became a little concerned after waiting almost ten minutes. At last, the sound of footsteps reverberated on the concrete floors. When she emerged from around the corner, she said, "Thank so much for the wine. I love your space here."

Sanders rose from the barstool. "I take it you found the bathroom okay."

She nodded. "Not a problem."

He followed Sara over to the door.

She grabbed the knob and turned around. "Do you ever have any events here?"

"I plan to have a grand opening soon. Although, I'm not sure how grand it will be."

She wrinkled her forehead. "Why do you say that?"

He snickered. "I'm not sure the Dallas art aficionados are ready to attend an art opening in the Richardson Core District."

Sara fished a business card out of the side pocket of her purse and handed it to him. "Maybe I can be of assistance."

Sanders studied the card. He read the first two lines out loud. "Sara Martin Public Relations."

She opened the door. Before exiting she said, "Check out my website and let me know if you think I can be of assistance."

He watched from the doorway as she slid into the driver's seat of a black BMW Z4 and fired up the engine. Sanders closed and locked the door.

She certainly drives a nice car. I think I'll check

out her website. This might have been a fortunate chance meeting. Or maybe it wasn't. How did she know where to find the bathroom? Has she been here before?

Chapter 10

After dinner, Sanders picked up his iPad and logged onto his Nonpareil.com account. There were three messages in his inbox. He opened the one from Kat. It read:

> Hey stranger, so sorry to cut our date short last Sunday. I was having such a lovely time before I received the email about my client's health. Anyway, I am much better now. Care to meet for dinner some night? VOOM is so hard to get, you never saw anything like it, I bet.
> VOOM!
> Kat

Sanders reread Kat's email several times.

What the hell does Voom mean? Is that another Cat in the Hat *reference?*

He accessed the PDF he had saved of *The Cat in the Hat* and read for what must have been the umpteenth time the entire children's book. There was no reference to VOOM. Sanders needed a cocktail. He mixed a CITRON vodka and soda and picked his iPad back up from the side table. A quick internet search of Dr. Seuss and VOOM led him to *The Cat in the Hat Comes Back*. He flipped through the pages online until he reached VOOM.

Of course, ZOOM was what Z cat had under his

hat that cleaned all the pink spots off the snow. Now what to do about her suggestion that they meet for dinner.

Sanders decided to ignore the Dr. Seuss reference and suggested the two of them meet for dinner the following Tuesday. He remembered she said she lived near Hillcrest Road and Campbell Road. Sanders knew Neighborhood Services Restaurant in Addison was only a few miles from that intersection, which should be convenient for her.

AT 6:45 P.M. TUESDAY EVENING, Sanders pulled his Spider up to the valet stand that stood a few yards from the entrance to Neighborhood Services. The dinner was scheduled for 7:00 p.m. He walked into the restaurant and scanned the restaurant for any sight of Kat. Satisfied she had not yet arrived, Sanders checked in with the hostess and made his way over to the bar, which ran almost the length of the restaurant. He had eaten many meals in the past perched on one of the stools at the bar.

The bartender recognized him and made him a Citron vodka and soda. He placed it on a napkin in front of Sanders. "Did I assume correctly?"

Sanders laughed. "You did indeed. Thank you."

He checked the time on his phone. It was 7:05 p.m. Out his peripheral vision, Sanders could see every time the door to the restaurant opened and shot a glance to check to see who was entering.

A few more minutes passed before the door opened and Kat bounded in. She was dressed in a casual white blouse and blue jeans. Her strawberry blond hair popped against her blouse. She said something to the hostess, who nodded in the direction of the bar. Kat surveyed the bar before she spotted Sanders and hurried over to where he sat. She plopped down on the stool next to him before he could stand up to greet her.

"I don't know why I bothered to ask the hostess if you had arrived," she said with a grin. "I should have assumed you would arrive early and be nursing a cocktail while you waited for me."

He smiled. "Yes, you're starting to understand my *modus operandi*."

Kat said, "So, how are you my second date from Nonpariel.com?"

Sanders laughed. "I'm doing pretty well, my second date from Nonpariel.com."

The bartender approached Kat. "What may I bring the lady?"

She leaned toward him, resting her elbows on the bar. "I think I'm in the mood for a glass of pinot grigio."

"Santa Margarita, okay?"

"Perfect."

Sanders said, "Everything going okay in your world?"

She nodded. "My client passed."

"I think I saw her obituary in the paper."

Kat glared at him. "Really?"

Sanders stammered. "Didn't you say her name was Davidson?"

Seeming nervous, she tapped a fingernail on the bar countertop. "Perhaps, but Davidson is a pretty common name, especially in a city as large as Dallas."

He nodded. "That's quite true. I'm sure it's just a coincidence."

The bartender returned with the glass of wine for Kat and placed it on a napkin in front of her.

She reached for it and said, "Thank you."

"My pleasure."

She paused. "But I will always have something to remember Glenda by." Extending her left wrist toward Sanders, she displayed a beautiful gold and diamond bracelet.

He leaned over to get a closer look. "It's stunning."

She stared down at her wrist. "It is, isn't it? She gave it to me as a keepsake."

"That's quite a gift, coming from a client."

Kat flashed a slight smile. "Yes, we became very close."

He took a sip of wine. "If I'm not prying, what was the cause of death?"

"Truthfully, a broken heart. Her husband passed away just a few months ago. But I suspect the official diagnosis will be congestive heart failure."

Sanders recalled that the obituary said donations to the Alzheimer's Foundation of America could be made in lieu of flowers. He wondered if that was why she was in hospice.

Kat took a drink of wine. "Yes. She otherwise was perfectly healthy for an eighty-seven-year-old woman."

He sighed. "How was her mental health?"

Kat studied his face. "What do you mean?"

"People of Mrs. Davidson's age often suffer from some sort of mental deterioration."

She took another drink of wine. "No, she was pretty sharp."

Sanders raised his eyebrows. "As I recall, the obituary said that donations could be made to the American Alzheimer's Foundation of America in lieu of flowers. I assumed that meant she probably suffered from the disease."

Kat's face tightened. "As her hospice caregiver, don't you think I would know if she had any mental issues."

"Of course. You indicated her husband recently passed away. Perhaps he suffered from Alzheimer's disease and that's why the statement was made in the obituary."

Kat took a drink of wine. "I don't know, Sanders. Can we possibly talk about something else?"

He patted her on the arm. "I'm sorry. I guess I was falling back into my attorney mode by scrutinizing all the details."

She smiled. "Well, I like you much better as an artist. In fact, I was on your website this morning."

Sanders breathed a sigh of relief. He was afraid

he had offended Kat. "Really? What do you think?"

"I think you're very talented. I love your bold abstract pieces. Several of them remind me of thunderstorms."

"I'm not sure I see the connection. That's the beauty of abstract art though. Different people can interpret a painting in different...". He paused mid-sentence and laughed. "Of course, you're reminded of thunderstorms. You're the woman who is only happy when it rains."

Kat gestured with her wine glass. "I'm glad you remembered."

The hostess tapped Sanders on the shoulder. "Mr. Pierce, your table is ready."

Sanders and Kat followed her over to the windows of the restaurant where Sanders preferred to sit. As soon as they were seated, Sanders said, "Have you been here before?"

She flipped her hair and looked around. "No, this is my first experience."

They each feasted on halibut. The conversation was light and upbeat. As soon as they finished, Sanders paid the bill and escorted Kat out of the door and to the valet stand. She stood by the valet stand.

As soon as one of the valets spotted her, he hollered, "I'll pull your car right up."

Kat flashed a smile.

Sanders said, "Didn't they give you a valet ticket?"

She shook her head. "No, that young man said he would remember me."

Sanders laughed. "You must have made quite an impression on him. I've certainly never received that treatment before."

Kat smiled. "One of my many talents."

"May I ask you a question?"

She pursed her lips. "Yes, as long as it's not about my work."

Sanders grinned. "No, not at all. I was just curious about your license plate."

Kat's eyes widen. "You are curious about Luna Wlf?"

He nodded. "Yes, does that mean you are the alpha female of the pack?"

She winked. "What do you think?"

The valet pulled her car up and waited by the open door for her. Kat leaned over and gave Sanders a quick kiss on the cheek. "Thank you. The dinner was lovely."

"You're welcome." He watched as she slipped the valet a ten-dollar bill and climbed into the driver's seat. She eased away from the curb and disappeared around the corner.

As Sanders drove back home to his apartment, he replayed the evening's experience in his mind. He had mixed emotions. On one hand, Sanders thought the evening went well. Both he and Kat had similar interests in common. The conversation was always lively and even spirited at times.

On the other hand, he kept thinking about the expensive bracelet gifted to Kat by her now deceased client. Was she telling the truth that Glenda Davidson did not suffer from Alzheimer's Disease?

If she did have Alzheimer's disease, then she might not have been mentally competent to make a gift of any nature. Have I gotten myself into another mess? Oh hell, I should stop seeing a villain around every corner. I'm just going to relax and enjoy myself for a change.

Chapter 11

Sanders arrived at his studio on Wednesday afternoon. He was feeling upbeat. Before settling into an afternoon of painting, he opened the top desk drawer in his small office. Sanders fished out Sara Martin's business card. He accessed the website listed on her card.

Other than stating her specialty was public relations for small businesses, it otherwise contained only generic information. There was no address, list of past clients, or testimonials of satisfied clients. He scoured the internet for any reviews or other information about Sara Martin but found nothing. Sanders flipped her card back into the desk drawer.

His afternoon was spent finishing an abstract painting he had begun several weeks earlier. He walked over to the couch in his studio, plopped down on it, and stared at his newest creation. Sanders jerked upright at the chiming of the doorbell.

Instead of walking straight to the front door, he went first to his office. He wanted to see if anyone was visible on his security cameras in front. Sara Martin leaned against the exterior wall, studying her cell phone. She wore a nice navy-blue pantsuit and again had her blond hair pulled back into a ponytail.

Through the intercom, Sanders said, "Hi, Sara. I'll be right with you."

Sara waved at the security cameras.

Sanders opened the front door. "Back to see some more art or have a glass of wine?"

Sara laughed. "I'm always up for a glass of wine."

He opened the door wider. "Please come in."

Out of habit, he locked the door behind them.

She gestured in the direction of the door. "Do you always keep your door locked?"

Sanders nodded. "Yes, I pretty much keep the place locked up when I'm here."

"Don't you think that might discourage some wealthy art collectors from coming in?"

He laughed. "If some wealthy art collector came visiting, I hope he or she would ring the doorbell." Motioning toward the bar, he said, "How about a glass of chardonnay?"

"Sounds yummy."

Sanders followed her over to the bar, where she perched on one of the barstools. He went behind the bar and retrieved a new bottle of Rombauer Chardonnay from the refrigerator. While opening the bottle he said, "So, what brings you into Interurban Contemporary this afternoon? I know it's not just for a glass of wine."

Sara leaned forward on the bar and studied the label of the wine. "Well, if I knew you were going to open a Rombauer Chardonnay, then I certainly would have come in just for a glass."

Sanders poured two glasses and slid one toward her.

"Since I haven't heard back from you," she said, "I wanted to see if you thought any more about me handling your P.R. for the art opening."

He took a swig of wine and swirled it around in his mouth before swallowing. "Yes. I even got on your website. But to be honest, there's not a lot of information on there."

Sara sighed. "I know. I desperately need to update it. However, it seems like there's always something else that takes priority."

Sanders smiled. "I sympathize. Updating my website ranks up there with unloading the dishwasher."

She chuckled. "I'm glad you understand. Let me propose this then. Would you consider letting my handle the P.R. on this event at one-half my normal fee?"

He raised an eyebrow. "Why would you do that?"

Sara took a drink of wine. "Because I haven't promoted an art gallery before. It would be a good learning experience and it might get my name out there with other galleries in Dallas. God only knows, there are a hell of a lot of art galleries in the Metroplex."

Sanders laughed. "You're right about that. May I ask what the typical fee you charge for handling the P.R. for this type of event?"

"Three thousand dollars. But in this case, I would do it for fifteen hundred ."

He rubbed his chin. "I didn't see any clients listed on your website. It only stated that you specialize in small businesses."

Sara set her half-empty glass on the counter. "To date, my primary clients have been independently owned small fashion boutiques across the Metroplex. I view promoting an art gallery event to be comparable to an event involving fashion."

Sanders nodded. "I can see the similarities." He gestured toward her glass. "Would you care for a refill?"

She glanced at her glass. "I shouldn't. I still have a couple of more errands to run."

"Do you have a template services contract that you use with your clients?"

She smiled. "Of course. I'll email it to you this evening."

"Perfect. I'll look it over and give you my decision tomorrow."

Sara grabbed her purse off the top of the bar. "May I use your restroom before I go?"

He reached for both empty glasses. "Of course. I think you know where it's located."

She winked at him. "Indeed. I'll just be a minute."

Sanders watched as she walked across the gallery floor and rounded the corner. He carried the two glasses and placed them in the dishwasher in the kitchen. When he returned to the gallery area, Sara was still in the restroom. He eased up on the end barstool and stared at his phone while waiting for her to return. Another five minutes passed before her footsteps reverberated on the concrete floor.

She rounded the corner at a quick pace with her

purse over her shoulder. "So, sorry to take so long. I had to respond to a text, which delayed me."

Sanders followed her to the door. She cracked it open and then whipped her head around. "Thank you so much for the wine. I so hope we can do business."

He grinned. "You're most welcome. I look forward to seeing your contract."

"It will be in your email tonight. Have a good evening, Sanders."

"Thank you. You, too." By habit and now instinct, Sanders locked the door behind her. He retreated to his office and shot a glance at monitor on the wall.

Sara was still parked in front of the gallery. She appeared to be rummaging through her purse. After a few more minutes, she tossed her purse over to the passenger seat next to her and backed her BMW Z4 out of the parking lot.

Why would she offer to handle the P.R. at half her fee?

Chapter 12

It was a cool and crisp Thursday morning in October. Sanders decided to begin his day with a cup of coffee and enjoy the view of downtown Dallas from his porch. When he finished his coffee, he walked back inside and plopped down in his favorite Eames lounger. Sanders opened his email on his iPad.

As promised, there was an email from Sara with an attached contract. Sanders pulled it up and glanced through it. The contract was brief but precise, laying out all the promotional activities Sara would perform. He thought about it for a few minutes and then decided he would hire Sara. He sent a quick reply to confirm receipt of the contract and to let her know he would return a PDF to her later today. Sanders targeted November 8th for the grand opening.

Sara shot an email back to him expressing how excited she was to represent him and suggested they meet next Monday afternoon to strategize.

SANDERS FINISHED PAINTING for the afternoon. He retired to his small office and accessed his laptop computer. In his mailbox was an email from Kat. They had not exchanged emails in several days.

Sanders opened it right away. She indicated she had a new client but was free Saturday night if he would like to get together.

He fired off a response and suggested dinner at 7:30 p.m. at Cadot, an old school French-themed restaurant located at the intersection of Preston and Frankford in far North Dallas. Kat would not have far to drive since she lived in the general vicinity.

Sanders hit the send button and glanced up at the security monitor on the wall. Sara's BMW Z4 was parked next to his Spider. She appeared to be talking on her cell phone. He checked his watch, it was 3:50 p.m. Their appointment was scheduled at 4:00 p.m. Sanders sighed. He questioned whether he had made the correct decision by agreeing to retain her. At least she was on time for the appointment.

Sanders and Sara spent an hour discussing various ideas on how to best promote the opening. There was several weeks until November 8th. Prior to leaving, Sara headed toward the restroom. The same as before, she was gone an inordinate amount of time. When she finally emerged around the corner, she said, "So sorry to be so long. I was just responding to some texts."

Sanders rose from his perch on a stool at the bar. "No problem. By the way, do you want a check? As I recall from the contract, I pay one half the fee upfront and the rest one day prior to the opening."

She smiled. "Thank you. You can give it to me when I stop by next time."

Sara hurried to the door and Sanders followed her. She exited and waved over her shoulder. "I'll be in touch."

Before closing the door behind her, he said, "Okay, goodbye."

Sanders walked into his studio and stared at the canvas he had painted earlier that afternoon. He pondered where he would go next with the painting. His cell chiming on the table next to him interrupted his thoughts. He reached for it and peered down at the screen.

In his message box was a text from his college roommate, Bob Portman. The two of them became fast friends as they sailed through their senior year at the University of Texas. Their paths diverged after graduation when Bob entered Austin Presbyterian Theological Seminary and Sanders entered Southern Methodist University School of Law.

How the hell did Bob track me down?

Sanders read the text and discovered that Bob had come across his website and was surprised to learn Sanders had become an artist. Bob invited him to meet for dinner sometime to catch up on everything in their lives. Sanders fired off a text suggesting Friday night.

Bob indicated that he was free since his wife was out of town. Sanders made no comment about his marital status. The two agreed to meet at 7:00 p.m. for a dinner of Tex-Mex at Mi Cocina in Highland Park Village.

I hope he doesn't ask about my wife. He probably doesn't know she committed suicide.

Chapter 13

Sanders located a space in the crowded parking lot that Mi Cocina shared with its neighbors in the upscale shopping center. He had not been to the restaurant since before his wife's death several years ago. As he entered the front door, he noted that little had changed over the years. The place teemed with affluent families from the Park Cities. He glanced over at the bar. It was packed two deep.

A booming voice behind him called out, "Charles Sanders Pierce."

He whipped his head around and spotted his old college roommate Bob Portman. The two shook hands.

Bob said with a smirk, "You haven't changed except for the fact you have no hair."

Sanders laughed. "That happens to some of us. By the way, how long have you had gray hair?"

Bob smiled. "That occurred around my third year in seminary. I decided to just embrace it."

"It suits you well."

"Thanks, Charles."

Sanders grimaced. "Just for the record, I go by Sanders now. But you're grandfathered in.

Bob patted Sanders on the shoulder. "A mid-life crisis thing?"

Sanders shook his head. "No, I made the change

on my last birthday. It's not a mid-life crisis unless I live to be a hundred and ten."

Bob laughed. "Well, you never can tell. Shall we get a table?"

The host led them to a booth near the bar area. "This is all that's available, Bob, unless you care to sit outside."

Bob said, "It's fine. Thank you, Miguel."

The two men were seated.

"You must come here often to be on a first name basis with the host," Sanders said.

Bob nodded. "Yes, I work just up Preston."

A server approach and took their drink orders. Both men ordered top shelf margaritas.

Sanders leaned in. "Are you a pastor of a church?"

Bob feigned a severe look. "No, I'm in a law firm." He laughed out loud at his own joke. "Of course, I'm a pastor of a church."

The server brought their drinks and placed them on the table. "Would you like to order now?"

Bob gestured toward Sanders. "Do you need some time to look at the menu?"

"No, I'm ready. May have the cheese enchilada dinner?"

The server jotted on her pad and then looked up at Bob.

"Mama's Tacos, and could I have some guacamole on the side?"

She nodded and walked away from the table as she wrote down the order.

Sanders held his drink up. "Cheers."

Bob tapped his glass against Sanders' glass. "Cheers."

Both men took a healthy swig of their margaritas.

Sanders said, "So, tell me about your job."

Bob set his glass down and rested his elbows on the table. "I'm an associate pastor at Preston Hollow Presbyterian Church."

"Really? I used to live near Preston and Walnut Hill. So, I drove by there all the time."

Bob smiled. "I don't suppose you ever dared step inside the church, did you?"

Sanders shook his head and took a swig of his drink. "No, I can't say I was ever tempted to go inside."

Bob laughed. "Still a faithless agnostic, I see."

Sanders tilted his head to look at him sideways. "This conversation is starting to sound like one of our college philosophical arguments."

The server set their dinners down in front of them. "Very hot plates."

The rest of the dinner was spent catching up on each other's lives. When the check arrived both men reached for it, but Sanders was able to grab it off the table first. "You're still a little slow on the draw, Bob, when comes to picking up the check."

Bob snickered. "You may be right. But thank you anyway."

Both men exited the restaurant and stopped to shake hands in the parking lot.

Bob said, "I'm really sorry to hear of your wife's passing."

Sanders sighed. "Thanks. It took a while for me to learn how to deal with it."

"I'm sure it did." Bob patted him on the shoulder. "By the way, are you seeing anyone?"

Sanders grinned. "I've had a few dates with a woman, but I don't know yet if it will develop into anything serious."

Bob smiled, "That's encouraging. What does she do for a living?"

"She's a hospice caregiver."

Bobs eyes widened. "That's a tough profession emotionally to be in. You get attached to your clients and then immediate death is inevitable."

Sanders grimaced. "That's very true." He paused as a thought crossed his mind. "She just lost a client that I believe was in your congregation."

Bob studied his face. "Really?"

"Yes, I remember reading her obituary in the *Dallas Morning News*. It said something to the effect that she was a member of Preston Hollow Presbyterian Church."

"Do you by chance recall her name?"

Sanders scratch his head. "I believe her last name was Davidson."

Bob's eyes flashed. "Yes, that would be Glenda Davidson. I conducted her funeral. Poor dear lady. She suffered from Alzheimer's Disease."

Sanders furrowed his eyebrows. "I now recall

seeing in the obituary they suggested contributions to an Alzheimer foundation be made in lieu of flowers."

Bob checked his watch. "I better run. Thanks again for dinner. Let's meet again soon."

Sanders poked him in the sternum. "And next time, you pick up the check."

As he turned, Bob waved and shouted over his shoulder. "Will do."

Sanders unlocked his car and slid into the driver's seat. He turned on the ignition and stared straight ahead.

Kat said her past client had no mental issues. But Bob said she suffered from Alzheimer Disease. That's consistent with the obituary. Did Kat steal that bracelet from some poor lady on her death bed? But as she said, Dallas is a big city. Maybe it was just coincidental that two women with the same name died on the same day.

Chapter 14

Saturday evening at 6:30 p.m., Sanders was driving north on the North Dallas Tollway. His music selection for the trip up from his apartment near downtown was nineteen sixties psychedelic. He knew all the words to all the songs from his adolescence but was not listening to them. Lost in thought, Sanders could not quit thinking about the discrepancy in Bob's and Kat's assessments of Glenda Davidson's mental faculties when she passed away.

He arrived at Frankford and Preston at 6:55 p.m. and found an easy place to park his Spider. As he walked to the entrance of Cadot, he scoured the parking lot, trying to spot Kat's SUV but failed to see it. He entered the restaurant.

The hostess greeted him. "Are you by chance Mr. Pierce?"

"Yes, that's me."

She motioned with her left hand. "Your party has already arrived. Please follow me."

Sanders trailed the hostess to a smaller dining area in the next room. As soon as he entered the room, he saw Kat seated at a two top table with her back to the wall. She looked up from the menu when they approached her table.

The hostess said, "Enjoy your dinner."

"Thank you." Sanders said as he slid into the chair opposite Kat.

Kat said, "Surprised to see me already here?"

He glanced at his watch. "You're right on time."

She laughed. "That's why I thought you would be surprised."

He smiled. "Well, it's true that I usually arrive for our date before you do."

She patted his hand. "I went ahead and ordered you a cocktail. I hope you don't mind."

"No, not at all." He gave her a wry smile. "What am I having to drink tonight?"

"Citron vodka and soda. In fact, it has just arrived."

The server set vodka and soda in front of Sanders, and a glass of champagne in front of Kat. "Shall I give you a few minutes to peruse the menu?"

"Please." He picked up his drink. "Excellent choice. Cheers."

They clinked glasses.

Sanders said, "How have you been?"

"Pretty good. I have been busy with work."

"So, you have a new client?"

She took a sip of champagne. "Yes, a Mrs. Tyler. Poor dear. I don't think she will be with us long."

He took a taste of his drink. "Sorry to hear that. Since she's in hospice, I assume she has six or less months to live."

Kat swallowed. "In her case, I would estimate we are talking weeks, not months."

He took a sip of his drink. "Must be something serious."

"She has a myriad of problems."

Sanders smirked. "Getting old is not for the faint of heart."

Kat smiled. "You can say that again. Shall we look at our menus?"

When she reached for her menu, Sanders noticed she was wearing a different bracelet tonight.

He said, "That's a lovely bracelet."

She glanced down at her wrist. "Yes, a friend gave it to me."

Sanders decided to change the subject. "What looks good to you?"

Kat closed her menu. "Dover Sole. You can't go to a French restaurant and order anything else."

He chuckled. "Okay, I'm sold."

After they placed their order, Kat said, "What's new with you?"

Sanders paused. "Well, I had a nice dinner last night with a friend I haven't seen for ages."

She studied his face. "Really?"

He smiled. "Yes, it was with my old college roommate."

She took a sip of champagne. "How did you happen to get together last night?"

"I give Bob all the credit. He tracked me down through my art website and emailed me. We met for dinner last night at Mi Cocina in Highland Park Village."

"That must have been fun catching up. Is he also an attorney?"

Sanders laughed. "Hardly. Bob and I roomed together our senior year at Texas. After graduation, he went to seminary, and I went to law school. We were good friends but diametrical opposites. Almost every night, we would get into these intense philosophical arguments."

Kat flipped her hair. "Does he live in Dallas?"

He took sip of his drink. "Yes. He's an associate pastor at Preston Hollow Presbyterian Church."

Her eyes widened. "I see." She paused. "Well, it's good you got to see one another."

Sanders furrowed his eyebrows. He was curious by her curt response.

Kat shot a glance over his shoulder. "I believe our dinner has arrived."

Was Kat's deceased client, Glenda Davidson, the one who was a member of that church? It sure seems like the dots connect.

Chapter 15

Monday afternoon, Sanders arrived at his building earlier in the afternoon. He was eager to begin work on a new figurative painting. Several months had passed since he last painted anything even remotely figurative. As Sanders was arranging the background paints on his table the doorbell chimed.

As had become his practice, he hurried into his office to check the monitor for the outside front security camera. Two men in dark suits stood in his parking lot, one near the front door while another man peered into the Sanders' Spider. A dark green Buick was parked on the other side of his car. He could just make out the license plate 357 975, with Exempt imprinted right under the number.

Sanders turned on the intercom. "May I help you?"

Both men looked up to the speaker under the roof line. The man nearest the speaker said, "I am Detective Powell, and this is Detective Thurman. May we come inside, please?"

Sanders was suspicious after his last encounter with two men a few weeks ago. "May I please see some identification?"

The man nearest the speaker grimaced but fished a badge from his pocket and held it up to the security camera. Sanders squinted at the monitor. It appeared to be a detective's badge, but he had no idea if it was real.

"May I inquire why you need to come in?"

"We'd like to ask you a few questions."

"All right. I'll be there in a moment." Sanders rose from his desk chair and made his way through the gallery to the front door.

God, I'm hoping I'm not making a mistake opening the door!

He cracked it open. "May I please see your badge again?"

Detective Powell was a heavy-set man in his early forties. He sighed as he held up his badge. "Satisfied?"

Sanders was still uncertain but felt he had little choice but to allow the men inside. "Yes, detectives. Please come in."

Detective Powell entered first, followed by Detective Thurman. The second man flashed his badge in the direction of Sanders before entering the building. He was younger than the other detective and lanky in build.

Sanders shut the door behind him and switched on all the lights in the gallery.

Detective Powell said, "You seem a little jumpy, Mr.—"

"Sanders Pierce. Detective, I've good reason to be a little cautious."

"Let's get some preliminaries out of the way first," Detective Powell said. "Are you the owner of this building?"

"Yes."

"How long have you owned it?"

Sanders shifted on his feet. "I purchased it several months ago."

Detective Powell rubbed his chin. "Judging by the sign outside and the paintings on the wall, I'm guessing you have an art gallery here."

Sanders wanted to respond with sarcasm but thought better of it. "Yes, I both paint and exhibit my work here."

"Do you use this space for anything else?"

Sanders shook his head. "No, that's all I use it for."

Detective Thurman said, "Mind if I have a look around?"

Sanders sighed. "Be my guest."

Detective Thurman took his time making his way around the gallery space.

"Now, let's go back to what you said earlier," Detective Powell said. "Why do you have reason to be cautious?"

Sanders rubbed his bald head. "Detective, I've been visited by some interesting characters since I purchased this place."

"Care to elaborate?"

Sanders glanced around. Detective Thurman was no longer in sight. He said, "First, some guy knocked on my door, asking to see someone name Reggie. I didn't let him in, but I told him over the intercom that there was no one named Reggie inside. He was insistent. A few minutes later, I saw him on my security monitor at the back door, trying to open it."

Detective Powell gestured toward the back of the building. "Do you record the activity captured by your security cameras?"

Sanders sighed. "No, I guess I never thought about doing that. I'm sure it has the capability though."

Detective Powell frowned. "Is that it?"

Sanders shook his head. "No, there's more. One day a strange note was left in my mailbox. It said something to the effect that the deposit had been made and that any further delays will be considered a breach."

Detective Powell raised an eyebrow. "You still have this note?"

Sanders paused to try to remember whether he had put the note. "I think I kept it. If so, it would be in my office. Would you like me to go see if I can find it?"

Detective Powell motioned with his left hand, granting permission for Sanders to leave. As he rounded the corner, the door to his personal restroom opened and Detective Thurman exited it.

Sanders hesitated at the door of his office and scanned the room. He was certain the detective had been in there. He walked over and opened the drawer in his desk where he kept his files. He removed an unmarked file and opened it. Paperclipped inside was the note that had been left in his mailbox. Sanders retraced his steps to the gallery.

The two detectives stopped talking when they spotted him rounding the corner back into the gallery space.

He walked up to the detectives and handed the page to Detective Powell. "This is the note."

Detective Powell read the entire note out loud.

"Why do you think someone left you this note?" Detective Thurman said.

Sanders shook his head. "I assumed it was left for the tenants who occupied the building before I purchased it."

Detective Thurman gestured with his right hand. "By the way, what's with all the strange plumbing in that bathroom in the rear?"

Sanders eyes widened. "I have no idea. The previous owner said the last tenants to occupy the building were photographers. Maybe they somehow needed the plumbing for their work."

The Detectives exchanged glances.

Detective Powell said, "You mind if we keep this note?"

"No, not at all."

Detective Powell handed the note to the other detective. He placed it a plastic bag and made some notations on the bag's label before slipping it into his coat pocket.

Sanders said, "There was one more thing I should tell you."

Detective Powell said, "Shoot."

"Two men confronted me outside one evening

when I was leaving. One of them opened his sport coat to show me a pistol in a holster. They made me let them inside to search the premises."

Detective Thurman said, "Did they say what they were after?"

"When I asked, one of them told me it was better if I didn't know."

Detective Powell said, "Did you report this incident to the police?"

Sanders shook his head. "No, they told me not to tell anyone. Since the ordeal ended peacefully, I decided not to contact the police. Detectives, can you please tell me the reason for your visit today?"

Detective Powell sighed. "Just following up on a tip."

Sanders raised an eyebrow. "A tip? What kind of tip?"

Detective Thurman said in a clipped manner, "Someone seems to think that drugs are being trafficked out of your building."

"That's completely insane." Sanders raised his voice. "Why the hell would someone think that. You can plainly see that nothing illicit is going on here."

Detective Powell growled, "Don't blow a gasket, Pierce. We have to follow up on what the department deems are credible tips."

He glanced at the other detective. "Let's let Mr. Pierce get back get to whatever he was doing when we arrived."

Both detectives gave Pierce their cards before

turning and walking toward the front door.

Sanders followed them. As he was leaving through the front door, Detective Powell turned around. "Give us call if you think of anything that might be relevant to our tip or if you are threatened again."

"You can count on that, Detective."

Sanders locked the door behind them and went into his office. He watched the monitors a few minutes as the men got in their car and then backed out of the parking space.

What the hell's going on here?

Chapter 16

Tuesday afternoon Sanders' Spider rounded the corner from Arapaho Drive onto Interurban Street. As he approached his building, he was relieved to see no one was parked in front. Sanders wanted to get a couple of hours painting before Sara arrived. She wanted a meeting to update him on her P.R. efforts to date.

The afternoon spent painting went smooth enough. He cleaned his brushes and checked the time on the wall clock. It was 4:30 p.m. There was time to enjoy a glass of Sonoma-Cutrer Chardonnay in his office before Sara was due.

He checked email on his laptop and noticed a message from Kat. The subject of the message was "All That Cold, Cold, Wet Day."

Intrigued, Sanders opened the email.

> Sanders, I want to see those heavenly views
> from your apartment that you described.
> I unexpectantly have tomorrow night off. The
> forecast for tomorrow calls for rain.
> What could be more divine than seeing the
> lights of downtown Dallas through sheets
> of rain. Are you free? Kat

He recognized the subject line of the email was a

sentence lifted from the first page of *The Cat in the Hat.*

I'm not sure what I think about her incessantly quoting Dr. Seuss.

Sanders fired off a response inviting Kat to come to his apartment for dinner on Wednesday night. He considered offering to come and get her but suspected she was more comfortable driving herself. When he was finished, he glanced up at the security monitor and saw Sara getting out of her BMW Z4. She was wearing a dark pant suit.

For the first time since he first met her, she did not have her hair pulled back in a ponytail. Sara rang the doorbell and waved up at the security camera above.

Over the intercom, Sanders said, "I'll be right there Sara." Sanders opened the door to let her in.

She bounded in. "I have some potentially good news."

He smiled. "I always like to hear good news, especially when it meets its potential."

She spotted his wine glass on the bar. "Enjoying some wine, I can see."

He gestured toward it. "Yes. Would you care for a glass?"

Sara walked to the bar. Without looking around she said, "I'd love a glass of whatever you're enjoying." She rested her bag on the bar and hopped on one of the bar stools.

"Excuse me. The bottle is in the kitchen. I will be

right back."

When Sanders returned with the bottle, Sara was sitting at the bar, staring at her phone. He poured her a glass of wine and scooted it in front of her."

"Merci Beaucoup."

"You speak French?"

Sara smiled. "You just heard my entire French vocabulary."

Sanders snickered. "Well, you nailed the 'thank you very much' part anyway. Tell me about this potential good news."

"Do you know who John Sparks is?"

He grimaced. "Not sure that I do."

She took a sip of wine. "Wow, this is tasty. Anyway, John writes a column for the Arts Section in the Dallas Morning News. I reached out to him about you opening a gallery here in the Core District among all the used car dealerships. Long story short, he was interested in perhaps writing a story about you being a pioneer gallerist in this area of Richardson. He indicated he wrote a similar article many years ago when the first art gallery opened in the Dallas Design District. Look what it's like today. There are over a dozen galleries located there now."

Sanders took a swig of wine. "That would be great, especially if the column appeared before our November 8th opening."

She clicked her nails on the bar top. "Precisely. However, even if it comes out after the opening, it should still generate some interest and bring people into the gallery."

Sara downed the remainder of her glass of wine. "I love this wine."

"Would you care for a refill?"

She nodded. "Absolutely."

Sanders refilled her glass and topped his glass off.

"Thank you."

He slipped the bottle into the small refrigerator next to the bar.

"My pleasure."

"I have been thinking, Sanders. If we're able to get people into the gallery, I really think it's a deterrent to have your door always locked. Surely, this area is not that prone to crime."

Sanders considered telling her about all the incidents that have happened including the visit by the detectives but opted against it. He leaned on the bar top. "Perhaps you're right. I'll consider doing that."

They visited another hour on strategy for promoting the upcoming opening and finished off the bottle of chardonnay. Sanders excused himself to go use the private bathroom next to his office. When he returned, Sara was staring down at her cell phone resting on the bar top.

She said, "I didn't realize it was getting so late."

Sanders glanced down at his watch. "Your right, it's almost six p.m. Shall we call it a day?"

Sara looked up from her phone. "Do you have any plans for dinner?"

He shook his head. "No, I'll probably drop in

somewhere near my apartment. That's one of the perks of living in Uptown, there are no shortage of restaurants."

She flipped her blond hair to the side. "Have you heard of Jasper's at Cityline in Richardson?"

He studied her face. "Yes, but I haven't driven up north to try it yet."

Her eyes brightened. "Would you care to try it with me tonight?"

Sanders smiled. "Sure. Do you think I'm dressed appropriately?"

Sara gazed down at his clothes. "You look fine. Very bohemian with your faded jeans bearing small paint spills. Slip on your sport coat and it's a perfect look."

He laughed. "Bohemian or perhaps more accurate, a well-dressed homeless guy."

She grinned. "So, are you game to go or not?"

"Sure, why not. Let me get my sport coat in my office."

She gestured toward the back of the gallery. "While you do that, I'll go freshen up in the bathroom."

Sanders fetched his sport coat from his office and returned to the gallery. He hopped on one of the barstools. He surmised that Sara would take her usual lengthy amount of time in the bathroom.

Like before, Sara did not return until about ten minutes had passed. She hurried around the corner with her heels clicking on the concrete floors. "So sorry to take so long."

She walked right up to Sanders. As he stood up from the bar, Sara gave him a hug.

Suppressing a gasp, Sanders said, "Not that I mind. But what was that for?"

She looked up at him and smiled. "I just wanted to thank you for giving me a chance to work on the P.R. for your opening."

He laughed. "You're doing it at half price. I'm the one who should be thankful. Come to think of it. Dinner is on me tonight."

Sara smiled at him. "A hug works every time. Now I got a free dinner out of you."

Sanders grinned at her. "So, that's your modus operandi."

She winked. "Let's go to dinner."

Sanders set the security alarm before they exited the building. "Would you like me to drive, or did you prefer to take separate cars?"

Sara patted his shoulder. "That would be great if you would drive."

They had a nice dinner at Jasper's. The conversation was light and covered topics from Sanders' career as an attorney to music and travel. He was not certain, but Sara seemed to deflect almost any questions about her past.

After dinner he drove the short distance back to his building in the Core District. Interurban was very quiet at night. The used car dealerships were closed for the day. The only business that appeared to be open was the local brewery located a few blocks north of Sanders' building.

As he wheeled the Spider into his parking lot, Sara said, "Your car is fabulous."

He parked his car in the space next to Sara's BMW Z4.

"Well, the Spider's impractical but I love it. It doesn't compare to your car, though."

She smiled. "I do love my car. It's a blast to drive."

They both got out of the Spider. Sara walked around the rear of the Spider over to where Sanders was standing. She placed both hands on his arms and reached up and gave him a peck on the cheek. "Thank you so much for dinner. It was quite lovely."

His eyes widened. He felt goosebumps on his neck. "You're very welcome. Have a good evening."

"You, too."

Sara scurried around the front of the Spider over to her car. Sanders watched as she fired it up. She waved before backing her car out of the parking lot.

Sanders slid back into his car. He drove back to his apartment. Traffic was light that time of night.

As he pulled into his parking space, his cell phone chimed. There was a text from Sara.

> Sanders, I just had to tell you again that I had a wonderful time. Thank you so much for dinner. I hope we can do that again soon.
> Sara

What just happened tonight? Is Sara coming on

to me? Surely not. She's at least twenty-five years younger than I am!

Chapter 17

6:00 p.m. Wednesday night, and as predicted by the weather pundits, the clouds opened over downtown Dallas. For the first fifteen minutes, the rain fell in quite intense sheets and then lightened up to a constant downpour. Sanders received a text from Kat, indicating she was stuck in traffic on the North Dallas Tollway. The traffic near downtown Dallas usually came to a crawl during rush hour. The rain exacerbated the traffic flow.

Thirty minutes later, Sanders was in his kitchen assembling the ingredients for what he hoped would be a perfect dinner of wine basted halibut. Three quick knocks on the door interrupted his train of thought. He washed his hands and rushed over and swung open the front door. His eyebrows shot up when no one was there.

A female voice from the left side of the opening whispered, "Zoom."

Sanders stepped out into the hallway and Kat stood grinning as she waved a bottle of Ramey Chardonnay in front of him.

Sanders chuckled. "Ramey Chardonnay is definitely worthy of a zoom."

Kat smiled. "Z Kat always comes through."

They hugged in the hallway.

He said, "I hope the traffic wasn't too intolerable."

"No, I decided out of the blue to take Uber so I wouldn't have to drive."

"Please come in." He clasped her arm and led her inside his apartment.

Her head swiveled around as she took in the ambiance of the apartment. She then spotted the view of downtown Dallas through the floor to ceiling window in the living area. Her mouth dropped open. "You weren't exaggerating. That's one stunning view."

"Yes, I never grow tired of looking out the window. Care for a glass of your Chardonnay?"

Kat flipped around to face him. "Of course. By the way, what's for dinner?"

Sanders gestured with his head toward the plate of halibut resting on the counter. "One of my specialties. Wine basted halibut."

Her eyes lit up. "Lovely. Chardonnay will pair perfectly with it."

He removed the cork from the Ramey Chardonnay and pour two glasses of wine. "I think you will like this wine. A beautiful lady gave it to me."

Kat chuckled, "You better think I'm beautiful or else you're history."

Sanders thought Kat did look most attractive tonight. Her light blue blouse, white jacket and matching blue jeans accentuated her shoulder-length strawberry blonde hair.

"I certainly don't want to be in the history books just yet. Listen, why don't you take your glass of wine and go enjoy the views from my covered porch while I get dinner ready."

She winked at him. "I'll take you up on that, particularly since it's still raining."

She walked from the kitchen towards the glass door that led to the porch, but stopped at the door and turn around. "What's this music you're playing?"

Sanders smiled. "Something I thought appropriate for the evening. It's Handel's Water Music Suite."

She toasted him with her glass before exiting onto the porch.

Sanders executed the preparation of the halibut almost to perfection. The conversation over dinner was light. They were becoming familiar with each other's interests and eccentricities. After dinner he suggested they finish their wine on the sofa which was situated to provide excellent views of downtown.

"That was a yummy dinner," Kat said. "Thank you so much." She leaned over and gave him a quick kiss on the cheek."

He twirled the wine in his glass. "Thank you for coming down here. I'm glad you took Uber, with all the wine we consumed over dinner."

She nodded. "Yes, I am a bit tipsy."

When she nodded, Sanders notice for the first time her diamond pendant neckless. It had worked its way partially out of the top of her blouse, which was unbuttoned at the top. "That's a beautiful necklace."

As she cast her eyes down at her chest, she sloshed her glass of wine. "I'm so sorry."

Sanders shot to his feet. "No problem, I will get

some paper towels."

He returned with the towels. "Did you spill any on yourself."

She grimaced. "No, I think most of it got on the sofa."

After patting down the sofa, Sanders said, "Would you like a replacement glass?"

"I thought we finished off the bottle at dinner."

From the kitchen, he called to her, "We did. I can open another bottle. However, it won't be as nice as Reamy."

She ran her hand over the moistened sofa cushion. "I don't want you to have to open another bottle of wine. Could I possibly just have a cocktail?"

Sanders eyes widened. "Uh, sure. I'm afraid I'm a little limited in what I can offer you, though."

Kat waved her hand over her head. "Anything is fine. You pick."

He mixed her a Citron Vodka and soda on the rocks and set it on the side table next to the sofa. Without asking what she was drinking, Kat picked the cocktail up and took a swig. Sanders eased back down on the sofa careful to avoid the moist wine spot.

"What were we talking about," she said, "before I drenched your sofa in a fine chardonnay."

He laughed. "I was just complimenting you on your beautiful necklace."

Kat took another drink of her cocktail. "That's right. Yes, it is lovely, isn't it?"

"It's spectacular. May I have a closer look?"

In a clumsy gesture, she pulled it out of the top of her blouse, enough that it was exposed. "It was gifted to me by my client, Mrs. Tyler."

Sanders concealed a gasp of surprise. "Wow, that was quite a generous and thoughtful gift. You must have been very close."

Kat stammered. "Well, I told you before, that it is the nature of hospice work. You grow very close to your clients during their final weeks or in this case, it was just days. In some cases, I am closer to my clients than their families. In other cases, there's no one else in their life. It can be very sad."

He took a final drink of chardonnay and set his glass down on the coffee table.

She spotted his empty glass. "Are you not going to join me for a cocktail?"

He shook his head. "No, I don't think I will have anything. So, what was the cause of death for the client who you cared for only days?"

Kat took a swig of her cocktail. "Cardiovascular Disease. Poor dear, her heart just played out."

"When did she pass away?"

"On Monday."

"How old was she?"

"I don't recall her actual age. But I know she was in her nineties."

Sanders leaned back into the sofa. "That's a long time to live. Was she mentally aware of her disease?"

Kat wrinkled her forehead. "Do you mean did she know she had heart problems?"

"Yes, the reason I ask is based on my own experience with my parents. My mother was mentally sharp until the end. My dad, on the other hand, had dementia, and I'm not sure he was cognizant of his other physical ailments. Both were in their early eighties when they passed."

She took another drink of her cocktail. "I suppose Mrs. Tyler probably had normal age-related mental deterioration."

Sanders gestured toward her now empty glass she still held. "Would you like me to take that from you and put it in the kitchen."

Kat handed him the glass. "Would you mind if I had another one?"

Sanders rose from the sofa and walked to the kitchen. He opened the freezer and reloaded Kat's glass with ice. Sanders started to pour vodka into the glass and paused. He said loud enough for Kat to hear him over the music, "You did say you were riding with Uber, right?"

She was staring down at her phone. "Yes, that's correct."

Sanders mixed her drink and returned to join her on the sofa. She took the glass from him and took a drink right away.

"Did I make it to your satisfaction?"

She nodded and set it on the table beside her. "Perfect, thank you."

Sanders was intrigued with Kat's admission that her client had age related mental deterioration. But she was comfortable accepting an expensive gift from her. He felt compelled to probe further.

"Tell me more about Mrs. Tyler."

Kat reached for her cocktail and took a sip. "Why are you so interested in my client?"

He leaned toward her. "I don't know. I just find people's life stories fascinating. After all, you were very close to her."

She stared down at her drink. "She was kind of a private person. So, she didn't dwell much on her past."

"Did she have any family? Did she have many visitors?"

Kat sighed. "She never mentioned anything about her family. As for visitors, no one came while I was there. I told you I was only her caregiver for a couple of weeks." She squirmed and wouldn't look at him.

Sanders decided to change subjects. He gestured toward the window. "It appears to have stopped raining outside."

She looked straight ahead. "Yes, what a pity."

Sanders snickered. "Oh yes, the lady who is only happy when it rains."

His comment provoked a smile from Kat. "Well, it's true. There is just something magical about when it's raining." Kat set her drink down and picked up her phone. "I suppose I better be going."

"What are your plans tomorrow?"

"I need to check tomorrow to see if I have any client referrals."

"How does the whole client referral thing work?"

She studied his face. "I get my referrals from various health insurance networks though my agency. There is a general health portal website setup for hospice workers. We can go in and review the requests for our services."

He raised an eyebrow. "Are you able to pick and choose whom you want to have as a client?"

Kat inched forward on the sofa, preparing to stand. "We have some flexibility. There needs to be a good match. Just like there are specialists in the health care profession, there are hospice caregivers who have more experience in dealing with certain health issues than others."

Sanders eased forward on the couch and stood up. "That makes perfectly good sense. I assume you have your specialties."

She stood up. "I usually get the clients who have heart disease, respiratory issues, and mental issues."

Sanders wrinkled his brow. "Would mental issues include such things as dementia and Alzheimer's?"

"Of course," she snapped.

He snickered. "I guess that's all the questions for tonight."

Kat pursed her lips . "I don't get you sometimes. You make me a delicious dinner and then give me the third degree about my job."

Sanders patted her shoulder. "I'm so sorry. I'm really interested in you and the wonderful service you provide for these people in their last days. It's the attorney in me. I get carried away. Please forgive me."

Kat hugged him. "You're forgiven. I am just a little tired and perhaps a little inebriated."

He led her to the door. "Let's contact Uber then and get you home."

They waited on the front sidewalk until Kat's ride pulled into the driveway. Sanders opened the door for Kat and gave her a quick kiss. "Let me know when you get home safe."

She smiled and nodded. He closed the door and watched as the car pulled away and took a right on McKinney Avenue.

It was quiet in the lobby of his apartment. He checked his mail while he was there and then caught an elevator back to the twelfth floor. Sanders walked out onto his porch and gazed at the view.

I really like this woman. She's quirky, beautiful, and very engaging. But is she also a thief? Surely, I'm mistaken.

Chapter 18

It was 4:00 p.m. Thursday on Halloween afternoon, and Sanders was getting a bit nervous about the opening on Saturday November 8th. He sat in his office, checking the usual art-related websites to see if his event was listed. The front doorbell chimed, interrupting his search.

Sanders glanced up at the security camera monitor. Sara waved at the camera over the door. He made his way through the gallery and opened the door. "What a surprise. Did we have a meeting scheduled?"

She smiled. "No, but may I come in?"

He swung the door wide open. "Of course. I was just searching the internet for the upcoming event."

She walked inside and flipped around. "That's why I'm here."

Sanders gestured with his right hand. "Let's go sit at the bar."

Sara smiled. "Does that mean you're going to offer me a glass of one of your stellar Chardonnays?"

He chuckled as he said, "That depends on why you're here."

She laughed. "I just want to do some last bit of strategizing."

She set her bag on top of the bar and hopped up on the end bar stool. Sanders pulled a bottle of Flowers Chardonnay from the small refrigerator next to the bar. "This should satisfy the requirement of a stellar Chardonnay."

Sara read the label. "Flowers? I'm not sure I've ever tasted that before."

He popped the cork and pour two glasses of wine. She took a sip from her glass. "Wow, I like this. It's very crisp and smooth."

Sanders leaned on the bar. "Yes, it's hard to beat. Say, any word from the *Dallas Morning News* columnist. What did you say his name was again?"

Sara set her glass back down on the bar. "John Sparks. No, sorry. I will try to follow up."

He sighed. "Sounds good."

She gestured toward the front door. "Are you ever going to start leaving your front door unlocked?"

He took a swig of wine. "Not sure I will do that. Maybe later."

"Well, you should at least post the hours you are open on the small pane next to the door."

He rubbed his bald head. "That's a good idea."

Sara picked up her wine glass and clinked it against his glass. "Thank you." She took a quick drink and set her glass back down. "Okay, let discuss the opening. Are you going to have a valet?"

Sanders shook his head. "No, I seriously doubt we will need one."

She wrinkled her forehead. "Where will people park then?"

"There are six parking places in front of my building." He snickered. "Don't you think that will suffice?"

"Sanders, we're going to have more than just a handful of people here."

He swirled the wine in his glass and stared at it. "There's plenty of parking up and down Interurban."

She took a sip of wine. "What about music? Are you just going to play Pandora over your sound system?"

"Yep. It is piped in throughout the building."

He noticed her glass was empty. "Care for a refill?"

She glanced down at her glass. "I would love another."

As Sanders refilled it, she said, "What about a bartender?"

He grimaced. "We need somebody to serve wine."

She picked up her glass. "I have a few contacts. Are you okay with thirty dollars an hour?"

Sanders nodded. "That's not a problem."

"Is all the art hung and lit the way you want it?"

He gave a quick survey of the gallery. "I'll tweak it here and there. I may add the piece I'm working on now."

She took a swig of wine. "May I see it?"

Sanders motioned toward the entrance to his studio. "After you." He followed her.

She entered and stared at his easel, then grabbed his arm. "I love it, love it, love it!"

He smiled. "Thank you. I guess it makes the cut to be in the gallery then."

"You're so talented." She gave him a peck on the cheek and clasped his hand. "Come, let's sit on the sofa and enjoy our wine."

When they were seated, she said, "I'm so glad I came in your gallery that first day."

He leaned back on the couch. "It looks like it worked out well for both of us."

Sara beamed. "I'm glad you think so." She started to say something then paused. "Sanders, I hope we can continue to see each other after the event."

His eyes widened. "You do mean on a business basis, right?"

She wrinkled her nose. "Not necessarily. Listen, I know you're probably hesitant because I'm younger than you. However, I've always been attracted to older men."

"Oh, so you're younger than me?" he said with a smirk. "I hadn't noticed."

Sara cackled. "Well, if you haven't noticed, then you shouldn't have any problem with our age difference."

She leaned over and kissed him on the lips.

He said, "I think I need a sip of wine."

She gave him some room to reach his glass. "So, you're not in a relationship or you?"

Sanders finished off his glass of wine and set the empty glass back on his coffee table.

"To be honest, I have had several dates with a woman I met on Nonpareil.com."

Sara listened as she stared at his face. "What's Nonpareil.com?"

"It's a dating site similar to Match.com."

She flipped her hair. "I see. Are you two getting serious?"

He shook his head. "No, it's too early. I can't really say if it will go anywhere or not."

Sara reached for her glass of wine. "Is she coming to the opening?"

Sanders sighed. "I mentioned to her that I was having an opening. But I haven't formally invited her."

She took a drink of wine. "So, she may or may not be there?"

He rubbed his head. "That's correct."

"Do you want her to come?"

"I suppose so," Sanders said with a chortle. "I need to at least fill up my parking lot."

Sara laughed. "You're being silly. I told you. You're going to have a nice crowd."

She glanced up at the clock on his wall. It was almost 5:00 P.M. "I should probably be going soon."

They both stood up and returned to the bar in the gallery.

Sara grabbed her bag. "I'm going to go use the ladies room before I go."

Sanders laughed. "So, it's known as the ladies room now, is it."

Before she disappeared around the corner, she shouted, "It is when I'm here."

He sat down on a stool at the bar to check emails on his phone. Fifteen minutes later, the sound of heels on concrete clicked as Sara made her way back into the gallery.

"Sorry to be so long. I got a text from a potential client and had to respond."

He raised an eyebrow. "You seem to always get a text or phone call while you are in the restroom."

She groaned. "I can't very well control that, can I?"

"I suppose not. It's Halloween. Are you doing anything fun tonight?"

She shook her head. "No, I'm just going to watch a movie on Netflix or something. What about you?"

"I'll probably do the same. I doubt if I will receive trick or treaters on the twelfth floor of my apartment."

Sara ran her hand through her hair. "I better run. How about we do dinner some night this week."

He rose from off the stool. "Sure. Sounds good. Did you have a night in mind?"

She smiled. "Tomorrow works for me. How about you?"

"That should work for me as well. Where would you like to go?"

"You live on lower McKinney, right?"

Sanders nodded. "Yes, I overlook Klyde Warren Park."

"How about Del Frisco's on Olive Street. I have this craving for a steak."

"Sure, that's literally right around the corner from my apartment"

"Perfect. Shall we say 7:30 p.m.?"

Sanders shifted his weight on the stool. "Sure.

Would you like me to make reservations?"

Sara hopped off the stool and headed toward the front door. "No, I'll take care of it."

Sanders followed her to the door. She gave him a kiss on the cheek. "Looking forward to it."

He smiled. "Me, too."

Sanders locked the door behind her and watched through the thin windowpane next to the door as she climbed into her BMW Z4. Without any hesitation, Sara got on her cell phone. He walked back to his office and plopped down in his desk chair. As she backed out and drove away, Sanders kept an eye on the security camera monitor in his office.

I can't help but be flattered. But something doesn't see quite legitimate about her developing a romantic interest in me.

Sanders strolled back into his studio and sat down in front of his painting. Whether or not Sara was sincere in her effusive praise of it, he was convinced that when finished, it would be hanging in the gallery for the opening.

He was tired and decided to call it a day. Sanders armed the security alarm and locked the door. He fired up the Spider, shifted into reverse to back out of his parking space. From his rearview mirror, Sanders noticed a man sitting in Buick parked in the lot directly across Interurban. As he drove past, he got a quick glimpse of the man's license plate. At the bottom of the plate was imprinted Exempt.

Is that guy a cop? If so, what's he up to?

Chapter 19

Sanders went to bed early on Halloween night. He even skipped his annual ritual of playing an ancient vinyl album with the soundtrack to *The Rocky Horror Picture Show*. Sanders woke Friday morning and laid in bed, pondering the day ahead.

Why did I agree to meet Sara for dinner? What about Kat?

He ate a quick breakfast and retired to his porch to drink a cup of coffee. He decided to send Kat an email.

> Hey Kat,
> Just checking to see how you are doing. I hope you were successful in securing a new client. Let's get together soon for dinner. Also, I know I mentioned my upcoming opening to you on November 8th. I wanted to formally invite you to attend. It begins at 7:00 P.M. As you can probably imagine, I have no idea how long it will last. Honestly, I just hope somebody attends. The public relations person I hired to promote the event is confident   we will get a good crowd.
> Take care,
> Sanders

Right away, Kat responded, indicating she had a new hospice patient under her care. She was scheduled to work primarily evenings. Dinner was probably not possible until she had someone who could cover for her some evening. She did say she would make every effort to attend the opening.

It was one of the few emails that did not make a reference to Dr. Seuss. Sanders did not know if that was a good or bad sign. He put on his runners to head out of his apartment building for exercise but came to an abrupt halt. The brief email exchange with Kat triggered a thought.

Last Wednesday, Kat said her client passed the prior Monday. If that's the case, then her client's obituary, if there was one, would probably be in the paper sometime earlier this week. I wonder if it will reveal the cause of death.

He rushed back into his apartment building, which surprised the concierge. "That was a quick bit of exercise, Mr. Pierce," she said.

Sanders rushed past her, shouting over his shoulder, "Change of plans."

When he returned to his apartment, he hurried over to the small built-in desk off his living room that he used as his home office. He accessed the website of the *Dallas Morning News* and pulled up the obituaries for the week. The website was organized by each day.

Sanders scrolled through the names listed on Monday. Kat said her client's last name was Tyler. There was no possible match until Thursday. The list on Thursday included a woman named Elsie Tyler.

He read the brief obituary in a hurry. There was no mention of cause of death or a charity to contribute to in lieu of flowers. The funeral was scheduled for 11:00 A.M. Saturday morning at Restland Funeral Home.

Sanders was very familiar with the funeral home. It had handled all the funeral arrangements when his wife passed away a few years ago. He rose from his desk and walked out onto his porch. There was a lot of activity in Klyde Warren Park. It was a beautiful sunny November day in Dallas. This was the kind of day that Kat would probably hate.

Sanders made up his mind that he was going to attend Elsie Tyler's funeral. He was not sure why, but thought he might learn the cause of her death.

AT 7:00 P.M., SANDERS EXITED his apartment building and walked two blocks north on McKinney Avenue. Del Frisco was an upscale steakhouse that occupied part of the first floor of a contemporary office building located at the northwest of Olive Street and McKinney Avenue.

The exterior of the restaurant consisted of floor to ceiling glass windows. The bar was almost always crowded this time of evening and tonight was no exception.

He was certain he had arrived before Sara and scanned the bar area for an empty stool. Sara was indeed there. She sat at the bar with her back to the entrance and was engaged in conversation with a man on her right. She wore a dark gray paint suit which accentuated her shoulder-length blond hair.

Sanders slid onto the unoccupied stool to her left.

The bartender approached him. "Sir, would you care for something?"

Sanders rested his elbows on the bar and studied liquor bottles situated above. "Do you have Grey Goose Citron Vodka?"

The bartender reached for a glass under the bar. "Yes, we do."

"Then I'll have that and soda, please."

Sara spun around on her stool. "Sanders, I didn't see you come in. Why didn't you say something?"

He smiled. "It looked like you were deep in conversation with this gentleman, and I didn't want to intrude."

"Don't be silly. Sanders, this is Nelson. We used to work together several years ago."

Nelson had thick, slicked-back hair and wore a crisp dark designer suit, white silk shirt open at the collar. He resembled the character, Gordon Gekko, the fraudster Michael Douglas played in the 1987 movie, Wall Street.

Sanders leaned over and extended his hand. He and Nelson shook hands.

Nelson said, "Pleasure to meet you, Sanders."

"Nice to meet you as well, Nelson."

"I was so surprised to see Nelson sitting at the bar," Sara gushed. "Anyway, we were just catching up a little."

Nelson nodded just enough to seem in agreement. "Yes, just catching up."

"Sanders is a new client of mine," Sara said. "We have an event coming up soon that I am promoting."

Nelson raised his cocktail glass. "I wish you a huge success. May I ask what kind of event?"

Sara patted Sanders' shoulder. "A grand opening for an art gallery. Sanders is a very skilled artist. He has a new gallery located in the Core District in Richardson. You know where that is, don't you, Nelson?"

Nelson stared at Sanders. "Yes, I know exactly where that's located."

Sanders snickered, "Well, you're probably one of a few."

Nelson furrowed his brow. "What do you mean?"

Sanders picked up his cocktail which the bartender had just delivered. "There's not a lot down there except for used car dealerships and repair shops."

"I'm very familiar with area," Nelson said in a chilly monotone.

Sara blurted out, "Why don't you come to the opening, Nelson."

Sanders' eyes widened,.

She twisted in her seat toward him. "You don't mind, do you, Sanders?"

Sanders felt nauseated. He had just met this Gordon Gekko character and had an instant disliking of him. In a terse tone, Sanders said, "Of course not."

Nelson gazed at Sanders, then at Sara. "I'll consider it. Listen, I've got to go." He leaned over and kissed Sara on the cheek and stood up. "See you kid." He laid a fifty-dollar bill on the bar, straightened his expensive suit coat, and slithered away.

Sara took a drink of her wine. "Sorry, Sanders. Nelson can be a little annoying at times."

Sanders took a sip from his cocktail. "He's not the most amicable person I've ever met. Where did the two of you work together?"

She flipped her hair. "Let's talk about something else. Nelson has intruded on our evening enough."

"Well, okay." He glanced at his watch. "Should we get our table?"

They were seated and both decided to order a petite filet mignon.

Sanders studied the wine list. "How about a bottle of Cabernet Sauvignon?"

"That would be lovely, Sanders."

He looked up and down the list. "How about a Camus?"

She unfolded her napkin and placed it in her nap. "Sure. I don't think I've ever had it before."

Sanders grimaced. "They've jacked the price up considerably, but let's get a bottle anyway."

They spent the better part of an hour talking about everything from the upcoming opening of the gallery to the recent weather. After dinner, they exited the restaurant.

"Where did you park?" Sanders said.

She pointed across the street. "I'm in that parking garage over there. How far is your apartment building from here?"

He smiled. "Two blocks south of here."

Sara grabbed his arm. "I have an idea. Why don't you walk me to my car, and I'll give you a ride to your apartment building?"

"Sounds like a plan. Besides, I would like to ride in your cool Z4."

Ten minutes later, Sara pulled her BMW Z4 into the driveway of Sanders' apartment. "Since we're here, why don't you invite me up to see the spectacular view you have of downtown."

He raised an eyebrow. "Sure. I'll let the valet know."

When Sanders got out of the car, a young man in a red coat approached the driver's side of the car. "Good evening, Mr. Pierce."

"Hey, Jason, how are you?"

He said, "Splendid" as he opened the car door for Sara.

She stepped out of the car. "Be gentle with my baby."

He smiled. "Yes, ma'am."

As Sara walked toward Sanders with her back to her car, Jason gestured a thumbs up in their direction. Sanders could not help but snicker.

"Did I miss something?" she said with a pout.

He shook his head. "No, Jason the valet was just having a little fun with me."

When they arrived at apartment 1206 on the twelfth floor, Sanders unlocked the door. He opened the door and followed Sara inside. His apartment was illuminated by the lights on the buildings in downtown Dallas that filtered through his living room window.

Sara made her way over to the window. "My God, that's absolutely stunning!"

Sanders flipped on a light in the kitchen. "Yes, I always keep the blinds open, so I'm greeted with that view every night when I walk into my apartment."

He joined her at the window. "Let's go out on my porch." He opened the door and they both went outside.

She said, "I just love all the city lights."

Sanders leaned on the railing. "Yes, I just wished I owned this apartment instead of leasing."

Sara joined him at the railing and placed her hand on top of his. "Thank you for dinner and show-ing me this amazing view."

He looked over at her. "You're welcome. My pleasure."

They stood there another few minutes. Then Sanders said, "Care to go back inside?"

"Sure."

He followed Sara back inside. "I would offer you something to drink, but probably not prudent since you have to drive home."

"Why don't we just sit on your sofa and visit it a bit."

Sanders gestured toward the couch. "So, what are your plans tomorrow?"

Sara batted her eyes. "Why, are you going to ask my out on a date?"

He laughed. "No, I was just making idle conversation."

She smiled. "I'm just messing with you. No, my usual Saturday routine is to sleep late, run all my errands in the afternoon, and have dinner with some girlfriends. What are your plans tomorrow?"

He leaned back into his sofa. "I will probably get some exercise in the morning and perhaps go to a funeral."

She studied his face. "Funeral? Was it someone you were close to?"

"No, just an acquaintance in her nineties who recently passed.

"At least she made it to her nineties. That's better than the average."

Sara scooted a little closer to him on the couch. "What about tomorrow night?"

"I will have a gourmet dinner in apartment 1206, followed by an exciting evening of Netflix."

She wrinkled her nose. "No date with the woman you met online?"

Sanders shook his head. "Nope."

"When is the last time you saw her?"

"Earlier this week."

Sara's eyes widened. "Really, was it a dinner date?"

He sighed. "You sure are interested in my personal life."

She put her hand on his thigh. "I just want to learn all about my competition. Tell me something about her. What's she like?"

Sanders chuckled, "Competition, eh? What's she like? That's a good question. She is a little eccentric."

"How so?"

"Are you familiar with the children's book, *The Cat in the Hat Comes Back* by Dr. Seuss?"

Sara nodded. "I'm sure I read it as a kid. Why?"

"Do you remember the Z Cat in the book?"

"Yes, the smallest cat with all the power to clean the pink off the snow."

Sanders sighed, "Kat's last name begins with a Z. I think she fancies herself as the Z Cat. She often ends text messages and emails with the word Voom which is what the Z Cat had under his hat."

Sara wrinkled her nose. "That is a bit eccentric."

He nodded. "Yelp."

"So, tell me about your last date."

"I made dinner for Kat earlier this week."

Sara's mouth dropped open and then snickered. "You have had two women in your apartment in the same week. You're quite the playboy, Sanders."

He blushed. "No, not at all."

"Will you make dinner for me some night?"

Sanders smiled. "Possibly. You never know."

She kissed him on the cheek. "I can be pretty persuasive."

"I'm quite sure of that."

"When is your next date with her?"

He shook his head. "We don't have anything scheduled."

Sara's phone chimed from inside her purse. She fished it out and stared down at the screen. "It's just a text from one of my girlfriends."

"I hope everything is okay."

Sara sighed. "Yes, nothing at all. But it's a tad late. I probably should get on the road."

Sanders stood up. "I'll walk you down."

Jason retrieved her BMW Z4 from the parking garage and pulled it up to the curb. She hugged Sanders and gave him a kiss on the cheek. "It was a lovely evening."

"Yes, it was."

Sara took a few steps toward her car and whirled around. "What's her last name anyway?"

Sanders wrinkled his forehead. "Who are you talking about?"

Sara winked at him. "My competition, Kat."

He laughed. "Zeman."

She rolled her eyes. "Kat Zeman? How charming."

Sanders watched her speed out of the driveway and turn north on McKinney Avenue.

Competition. She can't be serious!

Chapter 20

Saturday morning at 10:00 a.m., Sanders stood in front of the mirror on his closet door, staring at his reflection. He could not remember the last time he wore a suit and tie. Only one charcoal gray suit still hung in his closet. The rest were donated to charity.

Satisfied with his appearance, Sanders exited his apartment and rode the elevator down to the third floor where his Spider was parked. The funeral started in fifty minutes, which give him enough time to make the drive north up Central Expressway to where Restland was located.

He arrived at the chapel parking lot and with no trouble found a parking place. No more than twenty cars were in the parking lot.

As he climbed the stairs to the chapel, he felt a little sleazy attending a funeral for the sole purpose of searching for information concerning the cause of Elsie Tyler's death.

It was quiet in the chapel, as the few in attendance were speaking in hushed tones. Sanders located an aisle seat a few rows behind the others. He was relieved to see that it was a closed casket service.

The service started at 11:00 a.m. and concluded at 11:30 a.m. No one spoke other than the resident chaplain. He announced at the end of the service that a reception would be held in the room adjacent to the chapel.

A diminutive eighty-something-year-old woman with solid white hair greeted Sanders at the door. She beamed at him. "Thank you for coming. The family is over in the corner, if you would like to express your condolences."

Sanders forced a smile. "Thank you, ma'am." He ambled over to where the family was milling around.

A man in his seventies dressed in a black suit and silver receding hairline approached Sanders. He extended his hand. "I'm David Tyler, Elsie's son."

Sanders shook his hand. "I'm Sanders Pierce. My condolences to your family."

He smiled. "Thank you. She had a long and wonderful life almost to the end."

Sanders nodded. "As I understand, she lived to be in her nineties. We all would be so lucky to live that long."

"That's true. Yet none of us would want to spend our final few years the way she did."

Sanders narrowed his eyes. "Oh, I'm sorry to hear that."

David had an inquisitive expression on his face. "How did you know my mother?"

Sanders' face flushed as was prone to happen whenever he was uncomfortable. "My girlfriend was one of her caregivers. She spoke highly of your mother, so I thought I would pay my respects since she was unable to attend the funeral."

David's face softened. "That's very thoughtful of you. Excuse me while I make the rounds here."

Sanders ran the palm of his hand across his forehead. He was perspiring.

I wonder if I should get out of here before I make matters worse.

Sanders felt a tug on his coat sleeve. As he looked to his left, a woman in her seventies with black puffy hair that did not match the wrinkles on her face smiled up at him. "I'm David's wife, Lucy."

Sanders smiled. "Please to meet you, Mrs. Tyler." He extended his hand. "I'm Sanders Pierce. I'm so sorry for your loss."

She took Sanders' hand and held it for what seemed like an eternity to him. "Thank you for coming this morning."

He suppressed a sigh of relief when she at last released his hand. "Of course. I was sorry to hear of her passing."

Lucy shook her head. "Poor dear, she had suffered enough. It was time."

Sanders rubbed his chin. "If I'm not prying, what was the cause of her death."

Lucy sighed. "When you're in your nineties, there are usually multiple contributing factors."

Sanders was desperate to have an answer. "I heard she suffered from some type of congestive heart disease."

She leaned in as if about what she was going to tell Sanders was confidential information. In a hushed tone she said, "The official cause of death was heart failure, but her mind was gone long ago."

That statement hit Sanders like a lightning bolt. "Did... did she suffer from... some sort of dementia."

Lucy rolled her eyes. "The worst kind. She was in late-stage Alzheimer's. David's mother hadn't recognized him for months now. It was very sad. Her severe memory loss really upset David.

"I can imagine it's very disturbing when your mother no longer recognizes you."

Lucy squinted her eyes. "How did you know David's mother?"

Sanders sighed. "I didn't personally know David's mother. My friend was one of her caregivers. She always spoke highly of Mrs. Tyler. She was not able to attend today so I came in her place to pay last respects."

Lucy frowned. "Your friend spoke highly of David's mother? She must have been a caregiver back when the poor dear was more lucid. Even then, she was very difficult to manage."

Sanders felt a stress-induced pit in his stomach. "I... I... I'm sure caregivers are professionally trained to see past the patient's difficulties." He was uncertain if his response even made sense.

Lucy stared at Sanders. "What's your friend's name?"

He groaned. "Katherine, but she goes by Kat."

"Was she one of her hospice caregivers?"

Sanders nodded. "That's my understanding."

He looked at his watch as a distraction. "Mrs. Tyler, it was a pleasure to meet you. I have another appointment in an hour. So, I must be going."

"Of course, Mr. Pierce."

Sanders hurried out of the room. As he exited through the open door, he cast a glance back in the room. Lucy Tyler was still watching him.

When Sanders was outside of the funeral home, he sprinted to his Spider and slid into the driver's seat. His chest heaved, not from the brief sprint but from anxiety. He felt seedy. Leaning back in the driver's seat, Sanders closed his eyes.

I don't know what's worse, my attending someone's funeral for the sole purpose of gaining information or confirming that Kat is a liar and a thief. On the other hand, she was drinking heavily at the time she told me about the gifted necklace. Maybe, Kat confused Mrs. Tyler with a prior patient since her death was fresh on her mind. Who knows? What's my next move?

Chapter 21

It was Tuesday, November 4th. The grand opening of Interurban Gallery was four days away. Sanders arrived at his building at 3:00 p.m. He straight away went to his office and accessed the internet on this laptop. As he had done the day before, he checked which media had picked up the November 8th event.

The doorbell chime interrupted his search. Sanders glanced at the security camera monitors. Three men and a German Sheppard stood outside the front door.

He turned on the intercom. "May I help you?"

The heavy-set man said, "Pierce, this Detective Powell. We need you to let us in."

Sanders grimaced. "Yes, detective, I'll be right there."

Crap! What do they want this time?

He opened the door and recognized the detectives. "Yes, what is it, detectives?"

Detective Powell shoved a piece of paper into Sanders' chest. "This is a search warrant to search the premises."

Sanders' mouth dropped open. "What the hell are you searching for?"

"It's spelled out in the warrant," Detective Powell said. "To save you the trouble of reading it, we are searching for Methamphetamines."

"You mean like crystal meth?"

Detective Thurman said, "Exactly."

"You already know Detective Mark Thurman," Detective Powell said. "And this is Officer John Daniels and his canine partner, Charlie."

Sanders stepped back as the three men and dog entered his building.

Detective Powell said, "Officer, you and Charlie go do your thing. Mark, why don't you begin in the studio."

Detective Thurman made a beeline to Sanders' artist studio. Around the interior of the gallery, Officer Daniels followed close behind Charlie as he strained at his leash. Charlie sniffed the base boards and every so often reared up on his hind legs to smell the wall.

"Detective," Sanders said, "may I ask what triggered the need for a search warrant?"

"It's a felony in Texas," Detective Powell snarled, "to possess crystal meth."

Sanders rubbed his head. "Detective, the only reason I've even heard of crystal meth is because I watched the series Breaking Bad on television."

Detective raised an eyebrow, "Well, if that's true, you shouldn't have a thing to worry about."

"They're not going to tear the place apart, are they? I have my grand opening this weekend."

"Why don't you go have seat at the bar, Pierce, and relax."

Sanders did as the detective instructed but sat with his back to the bar so he could keep an eye on things.

Detective Thurman emerged from the artist studio and reappeared in the gallery. "It's clean, but Charlie will make sure."

A clanking of metal came from the direction of his office. Sanders assumed Officer Daniels and Charlie were going through his file cabinets. Detective Powell removed one painting from the wall, then proceeded to the others. He examined the front and back of each one before setting them on the floor to lean against the wall.

"Detective," Sanders said, "do you really have to take all the paintings down?"

Detective Powell ignored the question. Officer Daniels and Charlie remerged into the gallery and then disappeared around the corner where the studio is located. Detective Thurman used Sanders' ladder to inspect the exposed ductwork.

Sanders' blood was boiling. Officer Daniels and Charlie reappeared in the gallery.

"Let Charlie checked out the paintings," Detective Powell said, "now that they're on his level."

The dog led Officer Daniels counterclockwise around the walls, sniffing each painting. When they concluded with the last one, Officer Daniels shook his head. "Nothing. I thought he was onto something for a while, but it didn't pan out."

Detective Powell said, "Mark, did you check all

the bathrooms?"

He nodded. "With a fine-tooth comb."

Detective Powell sighed. "Pierce, do you know Reggie Perez?"

Sanders wrinkled his brow. "No, I don't believe I do. Why do you ask?"

"Perez was busted for possession of three grams of meth two days ago. During interrogation, he fingered 521 N. Interurban as his source. That's why we had to search your building."

Sanders eyes widened. "That's ludicrous, Detective. You know how long I've owned this building. It's not a source for anything illegal."

"Do you have many visitors?"

Sanders snapped, "You mean other than you and Detective Thurman?"

Detective Powell smirked. "Calm down, Pierce. We're just trying to do our job."

Sanders face softened. "I know. It is just frustrating."

"Would you please answer my question?"

Sanders looked up as he was thinking. "Not really. I'm not officially open as an art gallery. I told you about the two men who paid me a visit one day. I have a P.R. person, who is helping me promote my event this Saturday. But other than that, no one that I can recall."

Detective Powell looked at his partner. "Mark, you got any questions?"

Detective Thurman said, "Do you have a cleaning service or does anyone else have access to your building?"

Sanders shook his head. "No, I haven't gotten around to doing that yet. I set my security alarm every day when I leave. No one has access to the security code or my building."

"What about your P.R. guy?" Detective Powell said. "Does he have a key to the building?"

"My P.R. person is a woman. But no, she doesn't have a key or know the security code."

"You told us before that you don't record what the external security cameras monitor," Detective Thurman said. "Has that changed at any time since we were last here?"

Sanders pointed in the direction of his office. "No, I haven't gotten around to that either. You're welcome to check for yourself."

Detective Thurman sneered. "I did."

Detective Powell snickered. "Officer Daniels, do either you or Charlie have any questions?"

He laughed. "No, we don't have any questions."

Detective Powell motioned toward the front door. "Let's get out of Pierce's hair."

Sanders considered making a joke about his own shaved head but thought the better of it.

Detective Powell turned around after exiting the door. "Pierce, do you still have our cards?"

Sanders nodded. "Yes, detective."

"Give us call if you get any more unwanted visitors."

"Will do."

Detective Powell pulled at his ear. "Oh… and good luck with your opening. I'm sorry I had to take down your paintings."

Sanders forced a smile. "No problem, Detective."

He locked the door and went about the task of rehanging all the paintings. Sanders then flipped on all the gallery lights to make sure all of them were adjusted the way he wanted them. Satisfied, he retreated to his office.

Much to his surprise, the office area was not too disturbed from the search. He straightened up a few items on his desk and then accessed email on his laptop. An email from Kat indicated she was not able to get Saturday night off to attend the grand opening of his gallery. She suggested they have a glass of wine at her house Thursday afternoon.

Sanders was in the middle of typing a response when his doorbell chimed.

Who the hell is it this time?

He glanced at the monitor .A young mid-twenties woman with long black hair, white blouse, faded blue jeans, carrying a large tote bag over one shoulder was attempting to stare through the heavily tinted windows.

Sanders switched on the intercom. "Hello, may I help you with something?"

At the sound of his voice, the woman recoiled from the window. She scanned the top of the building, trying to determine where the voice came through.

"Hello, are you by chance open?"

Sanders deliberated on how to respond. On the one hand, he was not in the mood for visitors. But on the other hand, if he wanted the gallery to be successful, he should not turn away potential art collectors. "Yes, I'll be right there."

He unlocked and opened the door. "Sorry, I didn't realize the door was locked. Please come in."

She walked inside. "Thank you. I saw your listing on Dallas Art News about the opening on Saturday."

Sanders smiled. "Great, I'm glad some of the P.R. is working. By the way, I'm Sanders, the owner."

The woman extended her hand, and they shook hands. "I'm Grace. Pleased to meet you." Grace's head rotated halfway around as she took in her surroundings. "This is a nice space."

"Thanks, it suits me well."

"Are you the artist?"

"I am. Would you care for a glass of wine?"

She grinned. "If it's not too much trouble."

He gestured toward the bar. "Chardonnay or would you prefer a red?"

"Chardonnay is perfect. Do you mind if I start viewing the art up close?"

Sanders nodded. "Please, make yourself at home. If you prefer, you can set your bag on top of the bar."

Grace shook her head. "I'll just hang onto it. Thank you, though."

When he returned with two glasses of chardonnay, Grace was moving clockwise through the gallery. He handed her a glass.

"Oh, thank you."

"You're welcome."

She pointed at the painting in front of her. "I really like this piece. It reminds me of a cityscape."

The painting was abstract with vertical lines intersecting geometric patterns. Sanders stared at the painting, which reminded him he had not yet made labels for the paintings listing the size, medium, name, and price.

"Thank you. It's entitled *High Density*."

Grace took a sip of wine. "Nice."

"It's Rombauer. You can't go wrong with Rombauer."

Her eyes darted across the room. "Could I possibly use your restroom?"

Sanders' eyes narrowed. "Sure. Let me show you where it's located."

They both set their glasses on the bar, and she followed him to the back of the gallery and around the corner.

"It's that door there." Sanders pointed at the unmarked door while making a mental note to get a sign before Saturday night.

She scurried off to the restroom and he returned to the bar at the gallery. He perched on a stool and checked email on his phone. He saw his unfinished response to Kat's email.

So, Kat's invited me over to her house for a glass of wine. Do I tell her what I learned about Elsie Tyler?

That would be the end of any potential for a relation-ship. What if my suspicions are wrong?

Sanders fired off a brief email confirming Thursday afternoon and touching base prior to then.

After what seemed like an inordinate length of time, Grace emerged from around the corner, her heels clicking on the concrete floor. She hurried over to the bar. "Thank you. Unfortunately, I have to run."

Sanders stood up and followed her to the door. In seconds, she opened the door and exited the building.

He said in a tone laden with sarcasm, "Thank you for stopping by."

She waved with one hand without looking back. Sanders watched from the doorway as she slid into old Chevrolet Malibu with temporary license plates. He wondered if Grace purchased the vehicle from one of his used car neighbors. She sped off south down Interurban Street.

That was strange! She sure as hell didn't come in to see art!

Chapter 22

Thursday afternoon was a beautiful cool afternoon in Dallas. Sanders decided to drive with the top down on his Spider. He was not sure what to expect of the afternoon with Kat. He reached Campbell and Hillcrest at 3:50 p.m. for his 4:00 p.m. date with Kat. Finding a CVS Pharmacy at the corner, Sanders eased his Spider into the edge of the parking lot and entered the address she had emailed him into the MapQuest app on his iPhone.

Perfect, I'm only about seven minutes away. I wonder what her house is going to look like.

Back on the road, he turned the Spider onto her street and parked in front of Kat's house, a mid-century ranch situated on a corner lot. It reminded Sanders of the 1950s house where he grew up in Oak Cliff. In front of her door, he checked his watch. He was right on time.

Kat opened the door before he had a chance to ring the doorbell. "I saw you drive up. Please come in out of this dreadful sunny weather."

Sanders laughed. "I know you prefer rainy weather, but this weather is far from dreadful."

Kat smiled. "To each his own."

He stepped in her foyer and was struck by the huge abstract painting facing the door. "Cool painting. It certainly makes a statement."

"Thank you. Let me show you around." She led him through the living room. It was decorated with contemporary furniture. Various pieces of artwork adorned the walls lit to perfection by halogen can lights. They strolled through the den, which had a huge natural brick fireplace so characteristic of the 1950s. The furniture consisted of two mid-century modern Eames chairs. Artwork on the wall, although contemporary, evoked a mid-century feel. The only thing that screamed twenty-first century was a giant flat screen television attached to one wall.

Next, they entered the kitchen. It had been recently remodeled with the latest in high end appliances, an island cooktop and German cabinetry.

Sanders said, "What I've seen so far of your house is beautiful."

Kat smiled. "It's a work in progress"

His eyes scanned the kitchen. "Have you done all the updating?"

She nodded, "Yes. You should have seen the kitchen when I first moved in. The floors were that old linoleum flooring so popular in the 1960s. The cabinets and appliances were original to the house back in the mid-1950s."

His eyebrows shot up. "Wow, you've done a lot."

"Let me show you the media room."

Sanders followed Kat through another hallway off the kitchen which led to a huge room. The furniture consisted of two leather media chairs, a sofa, and an overhead projector.

"You have your own man cave," he said with a chuckle. "But I guess in your case, that would be a Kat cave."

Kat snickered. "Let's get a glass of wine."

They returned to the kitchen. Kat then opened a wine refrigerator and pulled out a bottle of Flowers Chardonnay.

Sanders eyes widened. "Nice choice."

She poured them both a glass of wine. "Let's go in the living room and visit."

They sat side by side on the sofa.

"How long have you lived here?"

Kat sighed. "Let me think. It must be about three years now. I moved in a few months after my husband passed away."

He took a sip of wine. "I see. Was your husband ill?"

She wrinkled her forehead. "Yes, Warren was considerably older than me. He had heart issues and ultimately died of a heart attack."

"That must have been a difficult time for you."

Kat shook her head. "No, he was a selfish narcissistic man. I should have divorced him long ago."

Sanders rubbed his chin. "Why didn't you?"

"Financial security. At least that's what I thought"

"What did your husband do for a living?"

"He was a jeweler."

Sanders took a drink of wine. "That would seem to be a lucrative profession."

She frowned. "That's what he led me to believe. He

always bragged about his prowess as an investor. I discovered after his death that he had only a few thousand dollars squirreled away in a bank. I don't know if he lost a fortune or never had one in the first place."

Sanders studied her face. "Did he have any life insurance?"

Kat shook her head. "Not a bit. The only asset he left me was his half-interest in our house in Plano. It was a very nice house and sold for more than I expected. That allowed me just enough money to buy this house, since it was so in need of updating."

He pointed around the room with a sweeping gesture. "But look at all that you've done."

Her face brightened right away. "Yes, and you know what I like the best about this house?" She shot to her feet. "Follow me and take your glass of wine with you."

He followed her into the hallway and then into the master bedroom. It was furnished with a maple contemporary platform bed, matching nightstands, chest of drawers and a flat screen television on the wall facing the bed.

"This room is gorgeous," Sanders said. "I can see why you like it best of all."

Kat pointed toward the bank of windows and a French door that led to the backyard. "That's what I like the very best. Let me show you."

She opened the door and stepped outside on the enormous cedar deck that overlooked an immense green space with a seating area and water feature.

"This lot is almost two thirds of an acre."

Sanders ambled to the edge of the deck to get a better look. "This is absolutely stunning. I would not have guessed it was this large from the front of the house."

Kat said, "Let's go enjoy our wine by my waterfall."

There was a cozy sitting area near the water feature complete with an outdoor fireplace.

Sanders eased into one of the chairs next to Kat. "I bet you spend a lot of time out here."

She gazed straight ahead at the water. "Yes, the cascading water on the rocks reminds me of rain."

He chuckled. "The woman who's only happy when it rains."

She nodded but did not respond.

"So, tell me about your new client."

Continuing to stare at the water, Kat said, "Her name is Mrs. Royce. She suffers from end stage renal disease."

Sanders groaned, "That's unfortunate. Is she elderly?"

Kat took a sip of wine. "She's in her early eighties."

"Does she have any family close by?"

"No. Mrs. Royce has had only one visitor since I've been with her. A pastor from her church dropped by one evening. She was sleeping so he didn't want to wake her."

Sanders rubbed his bald head. "I guess her husband predeceased her."

Kat set her glass down on a side table. "Yes, she

said he passed away over twenty years ago. Judging by her house, he must have been very successful. Also, you wouldn't believe this woman's jewelry collection. My husband was a jerk, but he did know jewelry and I learned a lot from him. I know stellar stuff when I see it."

His eyebrows shot up. "Really, how did you learn about her jewelry?"

She stared down at her empty glass. "Would you mind going and getting the bottle of wine?"

Sanders set his glass down. "Not at all. I'll be right back."

He walked back into the house. Instead of turning left in the hall toward the kitchen, he decided to turn right and explore the remainder of the house that he had not seen. The first door on his left was a guest bathroom.

It had been completely remodeled. Wood cubical shelfs were on one wall, displaying modern art glass vases and resort-type white towels. The shower was an extra large glass enclosure. Even the toilet was stylish and resembled what one would find in European five-star luxury hotels.

Sanders exited the bathroom and continued his exploration. The door on the right led to a guest bedroom and the door on the left led to another bedroom that Kat used as her home office. He hurried back down the hallway to the kitchen and retrieved the bottle of wine out of the wine refrigerator.

When he returned, Kat said, "Did you get lost?"

Sanders laughed. "No, sorry. I was just admiring your art." He refilled their glasses and set the bottle down on the end table. He leaned back in his chair. "Now, what were we talking about?"

She grimaced. "I don't remember."

"I do now. You were telling me about Mrs. Royce's fine collection of jewelry."

Kat picked up her glass of wine and took a drink. "Yes, she has some valuable things."

Sanders wrinkled his forehead. "How did she happen to show you her jewelry?"

"We were just visiting, and I complimented her on the necklace she was wearing. I told her my deceased husband was a jeweler and that I was an amateur connoisseur of fine jewelry. She insisted on showing me her entire collection. It's crazy. She keeps all these necklaces, rings, and bracelets in a shoe box in her closet."

Sanders took a drink of wine. "All very interesting."

Kat looked over at him. "I'm sorry to have to miss your event this Saturday."

"That's not a problem. I certainly understand."

"I hope it's a huge success. Are you all ready for it?"

He frowned. "Almost. I need to make some labels and put a sign on my restroom door. But other than that, I'm ready to go."

Sanders' phone rang from inside of his sport coat pocket. "I have to take this call. It's my security alarm company."

"Hello."

The voice on the other end of the line said, "Mr. Pierce?"

"Yes."

"The security alarm at 521 N. Interurban Street has been triggered. Are you on the premises?"

"No, I'm not there."

"We will notify the Richardson Police."

"Okay, thank you."

Sanders slipped his phone back into his coat pocket and stood up. "The alarm at my building was triggered."

Kat set her glass down. "Oh my. I hope it's a false alarm."

He stood up. "I apologize for cutting the evening short, but I need to go check things out."

They both rushed back into the house. Kat gave Sanders a quick hug and kiss. She called out to him as he bolted down her sidewalk, "Good luck, Sanders."

Sanders was grateful that traffic was light on Central Expressway He arrived at his building in only fifteen minutes from the time he left Kat's house. A Richardson police car was parked in the center parking space of his lot. Sanders pulled up alongside it. No one was inside the car. He got out of his Spider and stood on the sidewalk in front of his building.

A police officer appeared from the side of his building. The beam from the officer's flashlight froze on Sanders' face. He jerked his left hand in front of his face to block the light.

"It's okay, Officer, I own the building."

The officer lowered her light from Sanders' face but kept it aimed in his vicinity. She walked over to Sanders. "I'm Officer McKay, responding to an active security alarm."

Sanders took a step forward. "I'm Sanders Pierce. Did someone break in?"

Officer McKay gestured with her flashlight. "It appears somebody tampered with your backdoor. I could see some marking around the bolt lock. That door is rock solid. It's going to take more than that to get inside."

Sanders sighed, "That's good. My security system's pretty sensitive."

Officer McKay shined her flashlight at the front door. "Would you like me to go in with you to check to make sure everything is alright?"

Sanders shook his head. "Thank you, officer but I don't think that's necessarily."

"All right then. I'll wait here while you go inside."

The officer got into her car and turned on her headlights, which lit the interior of the gallery even through the heavily tinted windows. Sanders unlocked the door and switched on the inside lights. He scurried to the back door of his building. Nothing looked out of the ordinary. Sanders returned to the front, reset the security alarm, and exited the building.

When Officer McKay spotted him, she backed her car out of the parking lot. It took Sanders another thirty minutes before he arrived at his apartment. His phone chimed. Kat had sent a text inquiring about the security alarm.

He stared at his phone but did not respond. Sanders collapsed into one of his lounge chairs and replayed the events of the evening through his mind. He did not know what it was about Kat. She had this certain charisma that was so appealing, even though he was becoming more convinced that she was a thief. He picked up his iPad and searched the internet for potential salaries of hospice caregivers. The highest salary that he found listed in Texas was $41,000 a year.

How does Kat survive on that salary alone? How does she afford all those updates to her house? How does she afford all that super expensive furniture? What am I doing in this relationship? What's my next move?

Chapter 23

Saturday, November 8th, Sanders arrived at his building an hour early for his 7:00 p.m. opening. He parked his Spider in the rear of the building to free up all the parking spaces in front. The lock to the rear door was slightly damaged from the attempted break in a few nights earlier.

After a bit of jiggling, Sanders managed to unlock the door. He stepped inside, flipped on a light, jogged to the front, and disengaged the security alarm.

He spent the next twenty minutes touring the gallery, checking on lighting and labels. Sanders walked over to the guest restroom and admired the restroom sign he had installed yesterday. He went inside to make sure it was clean enough and had toilet paper and paper hands towels. It looked well stocked and smelled slightly of vanilla from an air freshener he had placed in the thin cabinet behind the mirror.

Sanders stared at himself in the mirror. He had bags under his eyes, the result of a sleepless couple of nights. His deepening concerns about Kat, coupled with tonight's opening, weighed on him. That morning, he even fished through his files and located the card of Detective John Gonzales.

The detective had saved his life last year when a fugitive named David Wayne Stapler stalked Sanders. He was the bait in a sting operation to capture Stapler. Sanders was supposed to engage a device that alerted the police if he encountered the fugitive. Sanders fumbled the device when the murderer surprised him in a tunnel underneath Maple Avenue in Dallas. As good luck would have it for Sanders, Detective Gonzales had anticipated Stapler would make his move in the tunnel and was able to intervene and make the arrest.

Sanders stared at Gonzales' card for several seconds, trying to decide whether to call him about his suspicions of Kat. He dropped the card back in the file, determined that he needed more proof.

The doorbell chimed and Sanders rushed through the gallery to the front door. He unlocked and opened the door. Sara stood there, dressed in an all-black pantsuit, black heels, white blouse, with the tips of her blond flowing onto her shoulders. She held a bottle of Champagne. She hurried inside. "This is for later on to celebrate."

Sanders laughed. "Pretty optimistic, aren't you."

She shrieked, "Of course, we're going to have a great crowd. I'm going to put this in the kitchen refrigerator." Her heels clicked on the floor as she walked through the gallery toward the kitchen.

Sanders started to relock the door but decided the gallery would officially be open for tonight's event.

Sara returned to the gallery and shouted from across the room, "Are you ready for tonight?"

He nodded. "I think so. I'm going to pour myself a glass of wine to ease some nerves. Would you care for a glass?"

She winked at him. "What do you think?"

The front door buzzed when it opened. Both Sara and Sanders looked around. A young man dressed in a black shirt and black jeans entered the gallery.

Sara said, "Our bartender has arrived."

At 6:50 p.m., all six parking places in front of the gallery were full. Fifteen minutes later, more and more people came through the door. At first, Sanders attempted to greet each person. After a while, he gave up on that endeavor.

Every seat at the bar was occupied. Hiring a bartender for the evening was definitely a good investment.

Two of his smaller abstract paintings sold the first thirty minutes after the official start time of the opening. Sanders made his way to the kitchen. He pulled a bottle of Ramey Chardonnay that he kept for himself out of the refrigerator and poured a glass. Sanders took a deep breath to enjoy a moment of solitude in the kitchen.

The bartender interrupted his privacy. "Hey, we're out of red wine. Do you have any more you want me to pour?"

Sanders pointed to the left kitchen cabinet. "There should be a half case up there."

The bartender grabbed two bottles from the cabinet and exited the kitchen in a hurry . Sanders decided it was time to return to the gallery. It was pushing 8:30 p.m., and people were still trickling into the gallery.

Earlier in the evening, the crowd was composed of middle-aged art enthusiasts and those in search of a free glass of wine. As it grew later in the evening, the composition of the crowd changed to a younger, upwardly mobile, trendy crowd. Sanders recalled experiencing the same type of phenomenon when he had a studio attached to a gallery in the Dallas Design District. To his surprise, the beautiful people did find their way to the Richardson Core District after all.

Sanders walked around the corner to where a storage closet and the guest restroom was located. The door was shut, while two young men talked outside of the closed door of the restroom. They ceased chatting when they spotted him.

Sanders said, "Is someone in the restroom?"

One of the men, dressed in blue jeans, polo shirt, and tan sport coat, said, "Yes, a woman just went inside."

"There's another restroom inside my office in the other part of the building. You're welcome to use it."

The other man said, "No, we're cool, thanks." His outfit was almost identical to the other.

Sanders raised an eyebrow. "Okay." He made a mental note to check the supply of toilet paper and paper hand towels before the end of the evening.

As he rounded the corner back into the main gallery, Sara waved at him. She stood next to a mid-thirties, tan-complexioned man dressed in gray slacks, black shirt, and a dark blue silk sport coat that glimmered under the gallery lights. When Sanders drew near, Sara said, "Sanders, this gentleman inquired about the painting over the bar."

"Great," Sanders said. "How can I be of help?"

The man gave Sanders a cool almost frosty, up-and-down look. "Tell me about that painting hanging there."

Sanders said, "Let's go over and take a closer look." He led the man behind the bar.

"This painting is titled *Concealment*. It's part of a series of paintings I'm doing with a certain urban influence."

The man was staring at Sanders instead of viewing the painting.

Sanders said, "Is something wrong?"

"No, go ahead." The man turned to face the painting.

Sanders rubbed his head. "Well, there's not a lot more I can tell you other than the medium is acrylic on canvas."

The man looked over at Sanders. "Why isn't it framed?"

Sanders sighed. "You might notice that none of the paintings in here is framed. They're all painted on gallery-wrapped canvas with their sides painted as well. As a result, they don't need to be framed."

The man never quit looking at Sanders.

"Any other questions."

In a gruff tone, the man said, "I guess not."

Sanders took a step away from him. "Okay, if you'll excuse me, I have to go check on something."

Sanders hurried across the gallery around the corner to where his guest restroom was located. He suspected the man was still watching him, so he did not look back. A young goth-looking woman with pale skin, jet black hair dressed in solid black, waited outside the closed door.

He said, "Is it occupied?"

She was gazing at her phone and recoiled almost dropping it.

"I'm sorry if I startled you. There's another restroom off my office if you would like to use it."

The woman shook her head. "No. I'll wait."

Sara walked up behind him. "There you are. You should be in the gallery. There's still a good crowd out there."

He turned around to face her. "This restroom certainly is getting the use tonight."

She tugged at his arm. "Come on, let's go."

As they rounded the corner into the gallery, Sanders scanned the room for the man he had spoken to about the painting. The man was nowhere in sight. "That man you introduced to me was certainly weird."

Sara wrinkled her forehead. "What do you mean?"

"I'm not sure. I don't think he had any interest in the painting."

Sara flipped her blond hair. "Why would he have me track you down if he wasn't interested in it?"

Sanders shook his head. "I don't know, he seemed to be sizing me up."

"I'm sure you're just imagining that."

"I need to go check on that restroom," he said. "As much use as it's getting, I want to make sure we don't run out of toilet paper. Could you check with the bartender on our supply of wine?"

Sara grabbed his arm before he could leave. "You stay in the gallery and check on the bartender. I'll take care of the restroom."

It was approaching 9:30 p.m. and the crowd was thinning out. Sanders made his way over behind the bar. "How's it going?"

The bartender said, "It's all under control."

"Do you need any more wine?"

The bartender shook his head. "No, we're good."

Sanders decided to see if anyone was in his studio. When he entered, he spotted the back of a young brunette woman dressed in blue jeans and light blue shirt. She was staring at the painting over his sofa.

Sanders said, "What do you think about that painting?"

The woman glanced around to see who was speaking to her. She was a beautiful young woman who appeared to Sanders to be in her early twenties.

She resumed gazing at the painting. "Are you the artist?"

Sanders drew nearer to her. "Yes, I'm Sanders Pierce."

The woman pointed at the painting. "I think it's

stunning. I'm trying to figure out how you got all that layering. It must have taken you forever."

He grinned. "I was in my twenties when I started it and I finished last week."

She looked over at Sanders. "Judging by the lines on your face, I would say it took you about twenty years to finish it."

Sanders laughed. "You're being kind with your estimate. But I'll take it."

"I'm Claire Stark."

"Pleasure to meet you, Claire. Thank you for coming to the opening."

"I'm glad to see an art gallery in the neighborhood." She leaned over the sofa to read the label next to the painting. "Layers of Civilizations. That's an appropriate title."

Sanders nodded. "I thought it fit the painting."

Claire pointed at the adjacent wall. "Those two orange paintings are similar to some of my work."

Sanders eyes widened. "You're an artist?"

"Yes. I'm only do it part-time, though. I've got to have a real job to pay the rent."

Sanders chuckled. "I understand. Do you have a website?"

"Yep." Claire fished a card out of her purse and handed it to him.

He read her card. "I'll check it out tomorrow. Do you exhibit your work anywhere locally?"

She shook her head. "No, I have some paintings currently on exhibit in galleries in Austin and others in Houston."

"I hope to start having regular exhibitions here featuring local artists. Maybe I can exhibit some of your work if you have an interest."

Claire smiled. "Of course, I'm interested. Check out my website and let me know what you think."

Sanders slipped her card in his shirt pocket. "Claire, it was nice to visit with you. I better go check on what's happening in the gallery."

"I understand. I need to be leaving soon anyway."

Sanders followed Claire back into the main gallery. He watched as she left through the front door. Sanders checked his watch. It was 9:45 p.m. He decided he would close the bar down and see if the bartender wanted to leave early.

The bartender said, "Nice crowd tonight. Let me know if you need any help again."

Sanders nodded. "Will do."

Only one couple remained in sight. They were a middle-aged, nicely dressed pair, positioned in front of a giant painting he finished several years ago entitled *Leaving New York*.

Sanders approached them. "Let me know if I can help you with anything."

The man said, "Thank you. We were just debating whether this painting would fit in our entry hall."

Sanders smiled. "It's the largest painting I ever attempted."

The woman said, "We love it. But I think it would overpower the space."

Sanders walked over to the hallway that led to the guest restroom. Sara rounded the corner just as he arrived. He said, "Is the restroom still Grand Central Station?"

She shook her head. "No. I think it's empty now."

Sanders gestured toward the gallery. "It looks like everyone has left. I guess the event is officially over."

They walked to the bar in the gallery. Sara said, "Where's the bartender?"

"I let him go a few minutes early."

She pointed at the bar. "At least he straightened everything up."

He smiled. "He should have cleaned it thoroughly, considering the tip I gave him."

Sara hopped up on one of the bar stools. "So, how do you think it went?"

"I sold two paintings and we proved that people would attend an art opening in the Core District. Based upon that, I would give it a B-plus grade. Anyway, shall we call it a day?"

She stepped down from the stool and gave Sanders a hug. "I think it was a nice opening. You will gain traction over time. How about a glass of champagne?"

Sanders forced a smile. "No, but thank you."

Sara released him from the hug. "Okay, shall we leave together?"

"No, I'm going to hang around for a little bit. I want to make sure the sales went through and then neaten up my studio."

They walked toward the front door.

Before opening the door, she said, "Let's get together in a few days and discuss where we can improve next time."

"Sounds good."

Sanders waited until she slid into her BMW Z4 before closing and locking the door. He walked into his studio and picked up a couple of empty wine glasses and took them to the kitchen. Tiredness started to settle in. Sanders decided he would just go home. He walked to the back of the gallery and made certain the back door was locked.

Sanders peeked around the corner where the guest restroom was located. He noticed three empty wine glasses were left just outside of the restroom. Sanders started to pick them but decided to check inside restroom first. He flipped on the light and walked over to the mirror above the sink. It was left slightly ajar from the cabinet behind it.

He pulled it open. The small air freshener he had placed in there before the opening was missing. Sanders scratched his head.

Why on earth would someone take the air freshener?

He was about to close the mirror when he spotted a small metal lever in the back on the shallow cabinet that he had not previously noticed. It was raised just a bit. Sanders pulled on it with his right forefinger and it clicked.

On the other side of the cabinet was a similar lever which was flush with bottom of the cabinet. It appeared to be a common wood fastener that held the joint together. He hurried back to his studio, grabbed a palette knife and returned to the restroom. With some work with the knife, he was able to raise it up far enough to get his finger underneath.

Sanders pulled on it and it clicked the same as the other one. He wrinkled his forehead, puzzled as to the purpose of these small metal levers. He tapped on the back wall of the cabinet and the back of the cabinet shifted from right to left like a pocket door, revealing a steel façade with keypad resembling that found on the front of a microwave.

Sanders was not sure what he had discovered in the secret compartment behind the mirror cabinet. He pulled his iPhone out of his coat pocket and took a photograph of his discovery.

I need to do some research on my computer to try to figure out what this thing is. But right now, I'm dead tired.

Sanders thought about leaving his discovery exposed and then changed his mind. After fumbling a few times with both levers, the wall at the back of the cabinet shifted from left to right, concealing the secret compartment. He pressed the levers flush with the bottom of the cabinet and closed the mirror.

As he was driving home, his thoughts drifted back and forth from the opening to whatever it was he unearthed in his guest restroom.

Chapter 24

Sunday morning Sanders rolled out of bed around 9:30 a.m. He brewed a cup of coffee and sat down with his laptop and pulled up his email. Scrolling through his mail, he found the email he had sent to himself last night containing the photograph of the object he found in the hidden compartment of his building.

Sanders studied the photograph for a while and then searched for something similar on the internet. Within a few minutes, he was able to ascertain that he had a wall safe concealed in his guest restroom of his building.

After a few more minutes, he learned his discovery was likely a very sophisticated digital wall safe. Sanders read everything he could find about these types of devices.

I wonder if I should contact the previous owner of the building. Surely, he was aware of the safe. I'll try and call him tomorrow.

MONDAY MORNING, SANDERS pulled out the file he kept on the 521 N. Interurban building purchase. John Axtell, the previous owner, had attached his business card to the Warranty Deed. He owned a mega plumbing supply company located on Turtle

Creek Boulevard in Dallas. Sanders dialed the number.

A female voice on the other end of the line said, "Axtell Plumbing, may I help you?"

"Hello is Mr. Axtell available?"

"May I ask who's calling?"

Sanders leaned back into his chair. "Yes, this is Sanders Pierce."

"Just a moment, I'll see if he's available."

After a long pause, a man's low voice at the end of the line said, "This is John Axtell."

"Mr. Axtell, this is Sanders Pierce, I purchased the 521 N. Interurban property from you several months ago."

"Yes, what can I do for you, Mr. Pierce?"

Sanders sighed. "Saturday night I was at the building and stumbled across a secret compartment behind a mirror in one of the restrooms."

There was a moment of silence. "Did you say a secret compartment?"

Sanders shifted in his chair. "That's correct. Where you aware of its existence?"

"News to me. That building was an investment property. I leased it out for about ten years before I sold it to you. I got tired of dealing with tenants."

"I see. Also, I discovered what I believe to be an upscale wall safe located inside the hidden compartment."

Mr. Axtell chuckled. "Maybe I should have spent more time in that building."

"I take it by your response, that you were not aware of the safe either."

"That's right. First time I've heard of it."

Sanders stood up from the chair. "I was hoping you could shed some light on the nature of the safe. Anyway, thank you for taking my call."

"You're welcome. Maybe you purchased a treasure trove along with a building. Good luck."

Sanders chuckled. "Thank you. Goodbye, Mr. Axtell."

Mr. Axtell hung up without responding.

Sanders opened the door and walked out on his porch. It was overcast and cool. Klyde Warren Park below had the usual Monday morning crowd.

What the hell am I going to do about that damn safe?

Sanders' phone chimed from inside his apartment. He rushed back inside and grabbed it off the coffee table. Kat sent him a text inquiring about Saturday night's opening and suggesting that they get together Tuesday since she had the night off.

Sanders sent back an email and suggested dinner at Neighborhood Services. He proposed they meet there at 7:00 p.m. on Tuesday. Kat responded, inviting him to come to her house at 6:15 p.m. for a pre-dinner glass of wine.

Sanders accepted the invitation but was conflicted because he was both attracted to Kat and yet convinced she stole from her clients. He had no empirical proof but just his suspicions.

SANDERS SPENT MONDAY afternoon searching the internet for someone who might have some expertise on wall safes. Much to his surprise, he discovered that legal safe cracking is a thriving profession in Dallas. Sanders accessed several websites before narrowing it down to one. He completed the online questionnaire identifying his problem.

Thirty minutes later, John K. Shapiro contacted him. He indicated he is normally booked weeks in advance but had a cancellation and thus an opening available 10:00 a.m. the next day. John agreed to come to 521 N. Interurban Street and give Sanders his professional assessment and estimate for cracking the safe.

Chapter 25

Tuesday morning at 9:30 a.m., Sanders pulled the Spider into the parking lot in front of his building. Interurban Street had a slightly different feel in the morning. Most of the used car dealerships and repair shops did not open until 10:00 a.m.

He brewed a cup of coffee and decided to wait in his office until John Shapiro arrived. Sanders accessed his email on his computer.

An email from Sara suggested they meet Wednesday afternoon to discuss last Saturday's opening. She proposed late afternoon so they could enjoy some of Sanders' exquisite wine. He was uncertain of Sara's prowess as a public relations professional but did feel she appreciated fine wine.

Sanders glanced up at the security monitor in his office. A black Porsche Cayenne SUV pulled into the parking space next to his Spider. The driver did not get out of the SUV for several minutes. Sanders surmised he was finishing up a phone call.

At last, the driver's side door opened and a tall man with neatly coifed silver hair dressed in a white pressed shirt, blue jeans, sport coat and cowboy boots emerged from the vehicle. The man bore a striking resemblance to the actor, Sam Elliot. He ambled up to the front door of the building. The man froze in the parking lot when he spotted the security camera at the top of the building.

Sanders flipped on the intercom. "Mr. Shapiro?"

The man nodded. "Yep."

"I'll be right with you."

Sanders hurried through the gallery to the front door. He unlocked and opened it. "Please come in, Mr. Shapiro."

John Shapiro strolled inside the gallery. He paused to fish a business card out of his shirt pocket and gave it to Sanders. "I take it you're the gentleman with the mysterious safe."

Sanders smiled. "Yes, I'm Sanders Pierce" Then he relocked the door behind them.

"Nice place you got here."

Sanders switched on the gallery lights. "Now you can see it better."

John's eyes scanned the gallery. "You the artist?"

"Yes, my art and my building."

"I saw your security cameras out front. Looks like you're well-protected."

Sanders nodded, "Yes, an incredible security system was already installed when I purchased the building. I had to hire a guy to teach me how to use it."

John raised an eyebrow. "You said on the phone that the previous owner didn't know anything about the safe."

"That's correct. This was strictly an investment property for him. He just leased it out."

John cleared his throat. "Most likely the person

who installed your elaborate security system also is the same one who installed the safe."

Sanders gestured toward the back of the gallery. "Shall we go take a look?"

The two men walked to the back of the gallery and to the guest restroom. Sanders flipped on the light and opened the mirror to reveal the shallow cabinet.

John pulled a small flashlight out of his coat pocket. "Do you mind if I take a look?"

Sanders stepped to the side. "No, please go ahead."

John held the flashlight in one hand and ran the other around the interior perimeter of the cabinet. "That's pretty sophisticated work. Whoever installed the hidden compartment knew what they were doing."

He turned around and looked at Sanders. "You figured out how to open this?"

"Yes." Sanders pointed to the right back corner of the cabinet. "That lever over there was slightly raised. I was able to get enough leverage with my finger to pop it up. That's the first time I noticed it was there. Every other time I opened the cabinet, that lever was flush to the surface like the other one."

John motioned with flashlight. "How do you suppose it got raised?"

"I had an event at the gallery last Saturday night. I suppose someone who used the restroom must have done it."

John stared at the lever. "I see. That makes sense."

Sanders leaned in. "Would you like me to open it?"

John shook his head. "Let me do it." He pulled a tiny flathead screwdriver from his coat pocket, the kind typically used on the screws of a pair of eyeglasses. John slipped it under the lever and popped it up. He followed the same procedure on the other side with the same result. He felt around the back of the shallow cabinet until it hit the mechanism that opens the secret compartment. The back wall slid from left to right, revealing the wall safe in the hidden compartment.

John shined the flashlight on the safe. He felt around the edges. "That baby is very secure."

Sanders said, "That was my impression as well. Is it digital?"

John scratched his head. "Yes, most definitely. This is a state-of-the-art European safe. My guess is that it would retail for about ten grand."

Sanders' eyes widened. "Really? Why would someone install an expensive safe in this building?"

John grimaced. "Whoever installed it has something they didn't want found."

Sanders rubbed his chin. "I wonder if there's anything in it?"

"Only one way to find out, Mr. Pierce."

Sanders tapped the exterior of the safe. "Are you able to crack it?"

John slipped his flashlight back in his coat pocket. "Yep. It's going to take a while, but I can open it. Do you want me to give you a quote?"

Sanders nodded. "Yes, please."

John pulled his phone out of his pocket and pulled up his calendar. "How much of a hurry are you in?"

"There's no urgency, as far as I'm concern."

"Unless someone cancels, I've got no openings until December fifteenth. Would you be receptive to letting me crack it some night?"

"Sure. That's fine."

John ran his hand through his silver mane of hair. "There's one other thing you need to know when I get it open."

Sanders wrinkled his forehead perplexed by the comment. "What's that?"

John sighed. "I'm ninety-nine percent certain that a signal will be activated when I crack the safe, alerting whoever owns this safe that someone is opening it without the proper combination. You better be damn certain that you want it cracked open and prepare accordingly for the consequences."

A chill shot down Sanders'spine. "Wow, I never considered that possibility. There's no telling who installed the safe."

"You give it some thought. I'm going to go to my truck write you up a quote on the job and an invoice for today's service call." As he walked toward the front door, he called over his shoulder, "I'll be just a few minutes."

Sanders went to the kitchen and brewed another cup of coffee. As he was rounded the corner that led to the gallery, the front door buzzed, and John Shapiro re-entered the building.

Sanders said, "Would you like a cup of coffee?"

John shook his head. "Thank you, but I don't touch the stuff." He handed the invoice and quote to Sanders.

Sanders perused the invoice and quote. "I'll write you a check for a hundred dollars to cover today's charge."

John smiled. "That works for me."

"Excuse me while I run to my office and write out a check."

"Mind if I look at your paintings while you're gone?"

"Not at all."

Sanders hurried to his office. He flopped down into his desk chair and pulled his checkbook out of the top drawer of his desk. He wrote the check and then picked up the quote. Counting labor and materials, the quote came to one thousand dollars. He rubbed his bald head.

Damn, that's a lot of money just to open a safe that's probably empty.

When he re-entered the gallery space, John was up close examining a large abstract painting entitled, *Choking on the Splinters*. Sanders had named it after a lyric from the song, *Loser*, written by Beck.

Sanders walked up behind him. "Do you like that painting?"

John said with a smirk, "I can crack any safe, but

I can't decipher this painting."

"It's called *Choking on the Splinters*."

John continued to study the painting. "I'll take your word for it."

Sanders smiled. "Here's your check."

"Much obliged." John tucked the check inside his coat pocket without looking at it.

Both men walked over to the front door. As John opened the door, he snickered, "If you hire me to open that safe, you better watch your back or else you could be choking on some splinters."

Sanders laughed. "I'll keep that in mind."

Chapter 26

Tuesday afternoon, Sanders was finishing off a sandwich in his office while watching a film clip someone had posted on YouTube of their dog. His front doorbell disturbed his lunch and entertainment. He shot a glance at the monitor and recognized Detective Powell.

Oh crap! What does he want now?

Sanders flipped on his intercom. "Hello, Detective. Can I help you with something?"

Detective Powell gazed up at the security camera. "I need to talk to you, Pierce."

Sanders sighed, "Okay, I'll be right there." He tossed the rest of his sandwich in the trash basket, ambled his way through the gallery, and cracked open the door. "What can I do for you, Detective?"

"Can I come in?" Detective Powell said in a gruff tone, "I have a few questions I need to ask you."

Sanders grimaced. "Sure, Detective. Come on in."

He opened the door wide, and the detective sauntered inside and glanced around the gallery. "How did your event go last Saturday?"

"It was fine." Sanders scowled. "Why do you ask?"

The detective stroked his chin. "Did you have a good crowd?"

Sanders studied the detective's face for some clue as to why he was here. "I had a decent turnout."

"Did you observe any unusual activity during the course of the evening?"

Sanders' eyes narrowed. "Unusual activity?"

Detective Powell shifted his weight. "Did you see a group congregating in the gallery or your parking lot?"

Sanders shook his head. "No. Can you please tell me what this is about?"

The detective fished a photograph out of his coat pocket. "Have you ever seen this woman before?"

Sanders examined the photograph. "It's certainly possible. I think she attended my opening Saturday night. If it's not her, it's someone who looks a hell of lot like her. She had the whole goth-look thing going on."

Detective Powell slipped the photograph back into his coat pocket. "She was arrested on a D.U.I. late Saturday over on Beltline Road a few blocks from here. The arresting officer found a gram of meth hidden in a pocket of her purse. When he questioned her about it, she became hysterical. Later, Detective Thurman interrogated her at the station. That's when this woman said she bought the meth from a man that was dealing at 521 N. Interurban earlier in the evening."

Sanders felt his hands get clammy. "Oh my! You're not accusing me of being involved, are you?"

Detective Powell frowned, "No. You don't fit the description. If the woman's telling the truth, the culprit is a twenty-something-year-old Caucasian male.

Unless you look old for your age, I would say you're pushing late-fifties."

Sanders forced a smile. "I guess there are some perks to getting older."

"Did you see a man who fit the dealer description doing anything suspicious?"

He shook his head. "No, detective. There were a lot of young men here during the evening. I didn't see anything out of the ordinary for an opening night of an art exhibition."

Detective Powell sighed, "All right Pierce. That's all for now. I take it you still have my card."

Sanders nodded. "Yes detective, I have it."

The detective plodded toward the door. Over his shoulder he said, "Call me if you think of anything. I don't care how insignificant."

"I will, detective."

Chapter 27

It was 6:00 p.m. Tuesday evening. Sanders texted Kat that he was struck in slow traffic on the North Dallas Tollway but anticipated being at her house around 6:25 p.m. The traffic at last opened north of Interstate 635, allowing him to arrive at her house.

Kat answered the door, holding two glasses of wine. Smiling she said, "May I offer you a glass of chardonnay?"

Sanders took the glass of wine. "That's excellent service."

As soon as he was inside, Kat hugged him and gave him a quick kiss. "It seems like ages since I've seen you. Come on in and tell me all about your opening."

They sat on the sofa in the living room. Sanders set his glass on the coffee table. "The opening went fine. We had a decent turnout."

Kat took a sip of wine. "Did you sell any art?"

He nodded. "Yes, two small pieces."

"That's good."

Sanders reached for his glass and took a drink. "There was one unusual thing that apparently happened."

She narrowed her eyes. "What do you mean?"

A Richardson detective paid me a visit today at

my building. He was following up on a lead. A woman who attended the event was arrested for a D.U.I. and the police found a gram of meth in her purpose."

Kat took a drink of wine. "What does that have to do with you?"

Sanders groaned. "She claims that someone sold her the meth at my opening."

Her mouth dropped open. "You're kidding."

"I wish I was. That's why the detective dropped by."

"They don't suspect you, do they?"

He shook his head. "No, thank God. The culprit was a young man."

Kat took another drink of wine and set her glass on the table. "That's bizarre if that woman is telling the truth. It's also quite brazen of whoever was selling the drug."

Sanders nodded. "Yes, but actually very clever. Who would suspect a guy of dealing drugs at an art exhibition?"

She gazed at Sanders' wine glass. "Would you like me to top your glass off?"

Sanders stood up. "Let me get the bottle and I'll top us both off."

"Thank you. I left the bottle on the island in the kitchen."

Sanders spotted the bottle of Chardonnay on the counter next to Kat's purse. As he reached for it, by accident he grazed her purse, knocking it on its side. A woman's diamond ring spilled out of the top of the purse onto the counter. Sanders eyes widened.

What the hell?

He snatched the ring off the counter and slipped it back into the purse and turned the purse back upright.

I hope she didn't hear that.

Sanders sauntered back into the living room. Kat was staring at her phone. He surmised that his actions went undetected.

AFTER DINNER, KAT INVITED Sanders outside. It was a damp cool November night. She suggested they make a fire in the pit outside. He lit a stack of pinon wood. The fire took hold in a few minutes. They sat side by side under some blankets.

Sanders said, "How's your client doing?"

She sighed. "Mrs. Royce is not long for this world."

"Did you say she suffers from End Stage Renal disease?"

She nodded. "Yes, poor dear."

He adjusted his blanket. "From what you told me before, it appears she had a good life. I believe you said that she had a nice collection of jewelry."

Kat looked over at him. "Yes, I forgot I had mentioned that to you."

"As I recall, you said she kept it in a shoe box."

She pointed at the fire. "I love the way pinon wood smells when it burns."

"Yes, very nice. Do you have to work tomorrow?"

She shifted in her chair. "Yes, tomorrow evening."

"Is administering medication part of your hospice responsibilities?"

Kat continued to stare at the fire. "Depends upon my client. When it's necessary, I do. Why the sudden interest in the specifics of my job?"

Sanders shifted in his chair. "I'm just interested in what you do. I bet that can be challenging when you have clients who have dementia or are just plain combative."

She tugged on her blanket. "Patients with Alzheimer's or dementia can sometimes be challenging."

"What about Mrs. Royce? Does she have any mental issues?

Kat looked over at him. "No, she's a sweetheart most the time."

Sanders pulled his arm out from under the blanket to check his watch. "I probably should be going soon."

"Big day tomorrow?"

He shook his head. "No, I'm meeting with Sara, and I also want to get some serious painting done."

Kat wrinkled her forehead. "Why are you meeting with her?"

Sanders sighed. "It was her idea. She thought it would be helpful to discuss what went right and what went wrong, so we can have a better event next time."

"I guess that makes sense. Sanders, do you mind

seeing yourself out? I'm going to enjoy the fire a little longer."

He stood up. "Of course not." He leaned over and kissed her. "I'll make sure the door is locked behind me."

Kat looked up at him. "Thank you for a lovely dinner."

Sanders smiled. "You're very welcome. I enjoyed the evening."

He walked up to her back porch and turned around. Kat was slouched down in her lounger. Sanders exited the house and fired up the Spider.

I so don't want to have bad thoughts about her. But...

Chapter 28

On Wednesday afternoon Sanders was fully engaged in painting. The Pandora app was turned to the Kraftwerk station. His spirits were lifted, and it was reflected in his work. Sanders was painting a rare surreal image of the Dallas skyline that came to him in a dream several months ago. He started it the morning after the dream but never could get inspired to continue it until today.

At 4:30 p.m., Sanders took a break and remembered he was meeting with Sara in a few minutes. He hurried to straighten up his studio and had just finished cleaning his brushes a second before the doorbell chimed. Sanders made his way through the gallery and opened the door.

Sara stood outside leaning against the front wall, dressed in blue jeans and a black blouse, with her blond hair pulled back in a ponytail. In fun, Sara sneered at him. "When are you going to start leaving your front door unlocked?"

Sanders shrugged. "Not sure. Would you like to come in?"

"Well, I don't want to stand out here all afternoon." Her large handbag brushed against him as she entered the building. She walked straight over to the bar and set it on the counter.

He followed her. "Would you like a glass of wine,

or do you want to get straight down to business?"

Sara smiled. "I thought wine was a part of getting down to business."

Sanders walked around to the backside of the bar. "I take that as a yes. Chardonnay or would you prefer a red?"

"Chardonnay sounds yummy. But first, I need to use the restroom. I have been running errands all afternoon." She grabbed her bag off the bar and headed toward the back of the gallery. Sanders watched her disappear around the corner before pulling a bottle of wine out of his refrigerator. He poured two glasses and perched on the end stool.

I wonder if I should tell her about my visit from Detective Powell concerning the meth related arrest and the tie to the gallery opening?

Sanders pulled his iPhone out of his pocket to occupy his time until Sara returned. He assumed she would take her obligatory fifteen or so minutes before returning. True to his assumption, the sound of her heels clicking on the concrete floor reverberated throughout the building as she rounded the corner into the gallery space.

She shouted, "Sorry to keep you waiting. I hope you started drinking wine without me."

"I had to taste it to make certain that it was good."

Sara walked past Sanders and placed her bag at the opposite end of the bar from where he was sitting. "Well, I trust that it's good."

Sanders nodded. "Actually, it's quite good."

She picked up her glass and held it up to the light. "What are we drinking?"

"It's a Ferrari-Carano Chardonnay."

Sara took a quick sip. "It's got a little bit of a bite."

He took a drink of his wine. "So, let's talk about the event."

"Overall, I was very pleased with the event.' She squinted. "I wish I could have gotten the columnist for the Dallas Morning News to interview you before it, but that didn't work out. What are your thoughts?"

Sanders grimaced. "I think it went all right. It was pretty well attended by many of the right kind of people. However, I'm not sure it was so special that people will want to return for subsequent events."

Sara patted his hand. "I disagree. From the conversations I had, people seemed really charged that you opened the gallery in this location."

He raised an eyebrow. "Perhaps, time will tell."

She took a healthy swig of wine. "You definitely got traction. I'm not sure what area we could improve on, except maybe media coverage and we can't control that."

"Maybe we should have reached out to more media, even those that don't typically cover fine art."

Sara nodded. "We can certainly do that in the future."

Sanders could not help but mentally note that Sara used the pronoun 'we'. She seemed confident she had a future promoting the gallery. "Can you think of any other areas to improve?"

She shook her head. "No. I know I always joke about it, but I do think you should leave your front door unlocked while you're here."

He took a drink of wine. "It's under consideration."

Sara grabbed his arm. "Can I change the subject for a few minutes?"

"Of course."

She smiled. "Have you seen Kat since the opening?"

He nodded. "Last night. We had dinner."

Her eyes widened. "How did it go?"

Sanders leaned forward toward the bar. "It went okay."

"Just, okay?"

He snickered. "We had a lovely dinner. It was a nice evening."

Sara giggled. "You don't sound convincing. Do you have another date planned?"

Sanders shook his head. "No, not at the moment."

She finished off her glass of wine. "In that case, are you free Friday night?"

He wrinkled his forehead. "Why do you ask?"

Sara winked at him. "Well, I'm in the mood for seafood. Would you be interested in going to Ocean Prime?"

He nodded. "You know what, that sounds good to me. I've never been there."

She stood up. "You'll love it. I hope to have them as a client one day. Would you like me top off your glass?"

"Sure."

Sara walked around the bar and retrieved the wine bottle from the refrigerator. As she was refilling their glasses she said, "Would you mind meeting me here at 5:30 p.m.?"

Sanders sighed. "I live within a few blocks from there. But if you prefer, I can meet you here."

She beamed. "Perfect. Thank you."

He had hoped by reminding her he lived near the restaurant that she would agree to meet him there.

Sara's phone chimed from inside a side pocket of her bag. She fished it out and stared at the screen. Her lips were pursed as she read a text. "I'm sorry, I need to respond to this client."

Sanders rested his elbows on the bar. "No, problem."

Sara spent the next ten minutes sending and receiving texts. Her face was drawn as she slipped her phone back into her bag.

"Everything okay?"

She nodded. "Yes, just a difficult man who's never happy."

He chuckled, "Sounds like you're describing me."

Sara did not acknowledge the joke. "I apologize. I'm going to have to run."

She scooped her bag off the bar and gave Sanders a quick kiss on the cheek. She paused before opening the front door, "I'll see you here Friday at 5:30 p.m."

Sanders waved from his seat at the bar. "See you then."

He finished off his glass of wine and took the glasses to the kitchen.

She's a curious one. Or maybe I'm the difficult one.

Chapter 29

Thursday afternoon in Dallas was cold and rainy day. It reminded Sanders of Kat and her strange obsession with rain. He had not had any contact with her since Tuesday night. The drive to his building took longer than usual due to the traffic slowed by the weather.

Sanders unlocked the door to his building and disarmed the security system. He flipped on the lights and started to relock the door but instead decided to leave it unlocked. Sanders walked inside his studio and searched through his art supplies for a thin palette knife. Satisfied with his selection, he walked to the guest restroom and flipped on the lights.

Sanders opened the mirror cabinet and took care as he slipped the knife underneath the lever on the right rear side. After a third attempt, he was able to pry it up ever so slightly. It was raised less than a sixteenth of an inch above the floor of the cabinet. It was not raised high enough to draw attention if someone opened the mirror cabinet.

He surmised that if someone in the future accessed the secret compartment, they would make certain the levers were returned to their flush position on the floor of the mirror cabinet when they were done.

He returned to his studio and plopped down in his chair to stare at his painting. The buzzer on his front door disturbed his thoughts. He sprang to his feet and hurried into the gallery space.

A young thirty-something-year-old man with dark closely cropped hair, wearing a black sport coat, white shirt and blue jeans, was standing in the middle of the gallery facing the back wall. Alongside of him stood a younger brunette woman wearing a buttoned up long raincoat and blue jeans. When they heard Sanders' footsteps, they both whirled around to face him.

The man said, "We saw the sign out front and thought we would check out the gallery."

"Great. I'm glad you stopped in."

The woman smiled. "Is this your gallery?"

Sanders nodded. "Yes and I'm the artist currently on exhibit."

The man said, "Do you mind if we just look around."

Sanders gestured with his right hand, "Please. Just let me know if you have any questions."

The couple walked to the right side of the gallery to examine a small abstract painting entitled, Downpour. Sanders went behind the bar and removed some wine glasses from the drawer and arrange them on the bar. It was subterfuge so he could remain in the gallery and keep an eye on the couple.

After a few minutes, the couple moved down the wall to the next painting. They were whispering to one another but not loud enough for Sanders to overhear. The couple moved to the next painting on the left rear wall. They were just out of Sanders' range of vision so, he walked from behind the bar to the center of the gallery.

"Let me know if you need any help," he shouted.

The man called out, "Do you mind if I use your restroom?"

Sanders pretended not to understand the question and walked over to where the couple were standing. "I'm sorry. I didn't quite hear what you said."

The man said, "I asked if you minded if I used your restroom?"

Sanders pointed in the direction of the guest restroom. "It's around that corner."

The man walked in the direction of the restroom without responding.

The woman beamed at him. "I love your work."

Sanders drew closer. "Thank you. Do you have a favorite?"

The woman wrinkled her forehead. "Not really. I like them all."

"I see."

The woman pointed across the gallery at the wall. "I changed my mind. That's my favorite. Can you tell me about that one?" She walked across the gallery in the direction she had pointed.

Sanders followed her. "Which one did you mean?"

The woman came to a halt in front of a small abstract painting. She motioned with her head. "That's the one."

Sanders stood to her side. "That one's entitled,

Imagine. Although abstract, it reminds me of a landscape horizon with a blue sky."

She nodded, "I can see that. Why did you name it *Imagine*?"

"*Imagine* was the title of a song written by John Lennon in the early nineteen seventies. I just thought it somehow was a good title for the painting."

"That's cool."

Sanders glanced toward the back of the gallery. "I hope your friend's okay."

The woman's eyes narrowed. "He's fine." She pointed at the painting next to *Imagine*.

Sanders walked over to the painting. He suspected she was trying to occupy his attention until the man returned. "That one's entitled *Burnt Orange Complex*."

The sound of footsteps echoed in the gallery as the man returned. He spotted them at the front of the gallery hurried over to where they stood. "Ready to go?"

The woman nodded. The man carried a small canvas bag that he was attempting to conceal from view. Sanders did not recall the man having a bag before he left for the restroom. The couple hurried toward the front door. Sanders allowed them to leave before he walked over and locked the door behind them.

Where did that bag come from?

Sanders jogged to the back of the gallery around the corner to the restroom. He swung to door open and flipped on the lights. Nothing looked out of the ordinary. Sanders opened the mirror cabinet. The lever on the right side he had left slightly ajar on purpose was now flush with the floor of the cabinet.

That man was inside the secret compartment, which means he was inside the safe! That's where the bag came from! What else is in the safe?

Sanders retreated to his studio and grabbed his palette knife and returned to the restroom. His actions were methodical as he slipped it under the right lever and left it raised, the same as he had done earlier.

Chapter 30

Friday morning was brutally cold in Dallas. From Sanders perch twelve floors above, Klyde Warren Park was almost vacant. An occasional business commuter crossed the lawn on foot from Uptown to Downtown, bundled up from head to toe. He decided to skip exercising and instead sat down to check email on his iPad. In his email was a message from Kat.

> It's time for a little rest. Mrs. Royce passed away last night. I have decided to take off next week to recharge. Let me know if you are available to get together for some delicious food somewhere. Also, I just read that a new Van Gogh exhibit opens Tuesday at the Dallas Museum of Art. Let's check it out. Hope you are doing well!
> VOOM!
> Kat

Sanders fired off an email suggesting the Van Gogh exhibit Monday night at a member only preview. He was a member and could bring Kat as a guest. She confirmed and the date was set.

At some point, Sanders knew he had to share his suspicions with Kat, if there was any possibility of them having a relationship. If he was wrong in what he suspected about her, she would be offended.

However, he felt compelled to risk it and get it off his chest.

The only other alternative was to walk away now. Neither alternative was very appealing.

FRIDAY AFTERNOON, SANDERS arrived at his building. He wanted to get a few hours of painting in before Sara was scheduled to arrive for their dinner date. The afternoon proved to be productive, and he was close to finishing his surreal painting of downtown Dallas. Sanders peeked up at his studio wall clock. It was almost 5:00 p.m. He cleaned his brushes and straightened up his studio. There was enough time for him to change into the clothes he brought with him to the gallery.

Sanders strolled through the gallery and back around to the guest restroom. He flipped on the lights and opened the mirror cabinet. The right lever in back was slightly ajar as he had left it the evening before. Sanders closed the cabinet and gazed at his reflection. The doorbell chimed. He flipped off the light and closed the door.

A quick check of his watch revealed that it was 5:20 p.m. Sara's face was pressed up against the tinted window, attempting to peer in. Sanders unlocked and opened the door.

She was dressed in a charcoal gray pantsuit and white blouse. "What took you so long?"

"I was in the back of the gallery straightening up

some things."

Sara walked in and kissed Sanders on the cheek. "How's my favorite artist doing?"

He smiled. "I'm doing fine. I'm close to finishing a painting."

Her eyes lit up. "Excellent. Can I see it?"

He motioned toward the bar. "Let's pour a glass of wine first."

Sanders followed her to the bar. She set her bag on the bar and perched on the bar stool at the right end. He reached in the refrigerator and pulled out a bottle. "I just opened this Flowers Chardonnay. Care for a glass?"

"Of course."

Sanders pour two glasses and slid one over to Sara. She picked it up. "Cheers."

They clinked glasses. "Cheers."

Sara squirmed off her stool. "Now may I see your painting?"

He said, "After you."

They walked over into Sanders' studio and stood facing the painting resting on the easel.

After a few seconds, Sara gushed, "It's stunning!"

Sanders chuckled, "Thank you. I'm glad you like it."

"What's it called?"

He shook his head. "I'm not sure yet. I need to come up with a unique Dallas related name."

She patted his arm. "How about *A Trinity Perspective*, since the viewer almost has to be standing in the middle of the Trinity River to have that perspective of downtown."

He creased his forehead. "You may be onto something there. I think I'll go with it."

Sara took a drink of wine. "I don't think I've ever named a painting before."

Sanders smiled. "Always a first time for everything."

She gestured with her thumb over her shoulder. "Why don't we sit on your sofa to finish our wine."

"Good idea. I always check out my painting from the sofa every day. It gives me a different perspective."

They sat side by side. Sara patted his thigh. "I'm so looking forward to dinner tonight. I'm ravenous."

He took a drink of wine. "By the way, I took your advice yesterday and left the front door unlocked while I was here."

Sara's eyes narrowed as she studied his face. "Did you have any visitors?"

Sanders nodded, "Yes, I had a young couple come in shortly after I arrived."

"Really? Did they buy anything?"

He shook his head. "No, I got the impression that they weren't here for the art."

She raised an eyebrow. "Why do you say that?"

Sanders sighed. "I'm not sure. It was raining yesterday at the time. Maybe they just wanted to escape the rain for a while."

"Did they look at the paintings?"

He nodded. "They did the obligatory tour around

the gallery pausing for a few seconds in front of several of the paintings."

Sara took a final swig from her glass. "Did they make any inquiries about the paintings?"

Sanders looked at her empty glass. "Would you like a refill?"

She shook her head. "I better not, especially if we have wine at dinner."

He looked at his watch. "Speaking of which, we probably should be heading out. Since it's Friday night, we will probably encounter some traffic on the tollway.

As they exited the studio, Sanders said, "Let me take your glass and put it in the dishwasher in the kitchen."

"Thank you. I'm going to run to the ladies room before we go."

Sanders paused before walking around the corner to the kitchen. He watched as Sara grabbed her bag off the bar and hurried to the back of the gallery.

It's certainly going to be interesting when I check the right lever in the mirror cabinet tomorrow. I hope she's not involved with whoever's behind that whole safe business.

TRAFFIC WAS LIGHT, to his surprise. Sanders and Sara arrived at Ocean Prime within a few minutes of each other. The conversation at dinner was upbeat and the seafood was exquisite.

The server set a black leather folder containing the check in the middle of the table. Sanders reached for it and flipped the cover back. He examined the bill and looked up at Sara, eyebrows raised halfway.

She laughed. "It's already paid."

Sanders set the folder down and raised the palm of his hands. "Really? You paid the bill?"

Sara smiled. "Yep."

"Thank you. That's very nice of you."

She patted his hand. "You've been very nice to me, Mr. Pierce."

He teased. "I could get use to this."

"Well, I hope I have many more chances."

As they exited the restaurant, Sanders clasped her arm. "Would you like to stop by my apartment for a few minutes before you head home?"

Sara gave him a kiss on the cheek. "I would love to, but I have to get home. I've got a breakfast appointment tomorrow and I need to prepare for it. I'll take a rain check, though."

He hugged her. "Sure, I understand."

The valet bought the Spider first. Sanders waved at Sara before sliding into the driver's seat.

He could not help but be smitten with her.

I pray that the right lever in that damn cabinet is still ajar when I get to my building tomorrow! Maybe I should head there right now.

Chapter 31

Sanders had a sleepless night and wished he had driven in the middle of night to his building. However, he dreaded what he might find. By dawn, he convinced himself to wait until Saturday morning before venturing up Central Expressway to the Core District.

At 9:30 a.m., Sanders made the right turn from Arapaho Road onto Interurban Street as he had done countless times. His hands turned clammy as he pulled the Spider into the middle parking space in front of his building.

Sanders went through his usual, methodical routine. He unlocked the front door and disarmed the security system. He switched on all the gallery lights. The entire gallery was bathed in light. Sanders strolled to the back of the gallery around the corner. He opened the door to the guest restroom and flipped on the lights.

Sanders paused and gazed at his reflection in the mirror. The bags under his eyes were more noticeable than usual.

He swung open the mirror and stared at the right lever. His heart sank and he groaned. The right lever was flush with the bottom of the cabinet.

Damn it, Sara's involved!

To postpone the inevitable, Sanders went into

the kitchen to brew a cup of coffee. Once his cup was brewed, he wandered into his office and slumped down into his desk chair. He opened his top desk drawer and fished out Detective Powell's business card.

Sanders took his time as he dialed the number on the card and put the call on speaker. He leaned forward, rested his elbows on top of the desk, and dropped his head into his hands.

On the third ring, a voice at the other end of the line said, "Detective Powell."

"Detective, this is Sanders Pierce."

There was a pause at the other end. Sanders surmised that the detective was trying to recall who Sanders was.

"Yes, Pierce, what can I do for you?"

Sanders took a sip of coffee. "Detective, I think I may have stumbled across something that might be relevant to your investigation."

"Really, what might that be?"

Sanders sighed. "I think it would more helpful if I could show you. Anyway, I discovered a hidden compartment in one of my restrooms. In the compartment is an elaborate digital safe."

"A digital safe? How did you connect that to my investigation of a meth dealer?

Sanders took a deep breath. "I think it's possible that the meth dealer is using the safe to store meth."

"Okay. Pierce, are you at your building?"

"Yes."

"I'll be there in about thirty minutes."

"All right, detective."

Sanders hung up the phone and grabbed a stapler from the top of his desk and hurled it against the wall. He didn't know which feeling was worse: anger or hurt.

Detective Powell turned into the parking lot in front of Sanders' building about forty-five minutes later. Sanders spotted him on the security monitor and rushed out of his office to the front of the gallery. He opened the door before the detective could ring the doorbell.

"Hello, detective. Please come in."

Detective Powell wore a crumbled gray suit that looked as though he had slept in it. His tie was crooked, and his white shirt protruded over his belt. He nodded. "Pierce."

The detective lumbered inside the building. "Show me this mysterious safe."

Sanders motioned with his head. "This way. It's in the restroom I make available for my guests."

The detective followed Sanders to the restroom. Sanders opened the door and flipped on the lights. He pointed at the mirror. "The secret compartment is located behind the shallow mirror cabinet."

Sanders opened the cabinet and switched on his iPhone light. He directed the beam at the right back of the cabinet. "See that metal lever embedded in the floor of the cabinet."

Detective Powell leaned forward and squinted his

eyes. "Yes."

"The night of my opening, I was cleaning up afterwards. I opened the mirror cabinet and noticed an air freshener I had placed inside was missing. As I pondering what happened to it, I noticed the right lever was slightly raised from the floor. I was able to pry it up and then I pried up the other lever of the left side. When I raised the second lever and pressed the back left side, the back of the cabinet slid to the side, revealing a wall safe in the secret compartment."

"Show me."

"I need to get my palette knife."

Detective Powell held up his hand to stop Sanders. He reached in his coat pocket and pulled out a pocketknife. "Will this work?"

Sanders nodded. "That should do the trick."

The detective watched as Sanders pried up the right lever followed by the left lever and then pressed the back wall on the left side. The back wall of the shallow cabinet shifted from left to right and the wall safe appeared.

Detective Powell rubbed his chin. "You knew nothing about this safe?"

"That's correct. I even called the guy who previously owned the building to see if he was aware of it."

"Was he?"

Sanders shook his head. "No, it was news to him."

"Why do you think it is related to my meth investigation?"

Sanders rubbed his head. "During my event, I

noticed this restroom seemed to always have someone outside waiting to get in. I didn't think anything of it because we were serving wine. I think someone was dealing meth that night out of the restroom."

Detective Powell narrowed his eyes. "That's quite an assumption, don't you think?"

Sanders sighed. "There's more to the story. I am pretty certain the woman I hired to help promote the event is involved. I think she was trying to get close to me so she would have easy access to the safe as needed."

Detective shifted his weight. "What makes you think that?"

"This woman shows up at the gallery one day out of the blue. It turns out she was in public relations or that's what she led me to believe. She ultimately convinced me to let her do the P.R. for half her normal fee. Sara Martin is her name, a lovely woman in her early thirties. She feigned having a romantic interest in me to gain access to the safe. I'm more than twenty years older than she is. It just didn't seem genuine to me, but I have to admit to being flattered."

Detective Powell raised an eyebrow. "Is that all you got?"

Sanders shook his head. "No. There's more. Every time Sara was here, she spent an inordinate amount of time in the restroom. She always used the excuse that she got a call or text which is the reason she stayed in there so long."

He paused as if he had lost his train of thought.

"Let me back up a bit. When I discovered the safe, I found on the internet a man named John Shapiro, who is a professional safe cracker. Mr. Shapiro came and gave me an estimate for cracking it. He described the mechanism for accessing the hidden compartment as being very sophisticated. The digital wall safe is even more elaborate."

Detective Powell leaned in. "I don't suppose he opened it?"

"No, he gave me an estimate. He did say he was very certain that if he cracks it open, it will send off a signal to whoever is responsible for it. Now that seems pretty sophisticated and something a drug dealer might be behind."

Detective Powell nodded. "That's possible. Anything else?"

Sanders sighed. "Yes. Here's the clincher. I decided to set a trap. I pulled the right lever slightly above the floor so you wouldn't necessarily notice it was raised. I check on it every time someone uses the restroom."

He paused, as if to collect his thoughts. "Anyway, a young couple came in here one afternoon last week. The man asked to use the restroom. When he returned, he was carrying a small canvas bag, holding it close by his side in an attempt to conceal it. He didn't have a bag with him when he entered the restroom. After they left in a hurry, I checked the right lever in the cabinet, and it was flush with the floor of the mirror cabinet. I suspect the bag and its contents came from within the safe."

"You never have seen the bag anywhere before?"

Sanders shook his head. "No. Anyway, I set the trap again yesterday. The only visitor all day was Sara. We had a date to go to dinner, so she met me here at around 5:30 p.m. As was her custom, she went to use the restroom before we left. The first thing this morning when I arrived was to check on the lever."

Sanders took a deep breath. "It was flush with the floor."

Detective Powell rubbed his nose. "Was your security system armed last night?"

Sanders nodded. "Yes, I turned it off when I entered the building this morning."

"Do you know where this Sara Martin works or lives?"

"No. I don't know."

"But you have her phone number?"

Sanders motioned with his head. "Yes, I can also give you the business card she gave me."

"Most likely she's using a fake name anyway. Do you think she has any clue you suspect her?"

Sanders shook his head. "I'm positive she doesn't know."

Detective Powell eyes widened. "Good. Are you expecting her show up anytime?"

"No. We have nothing formal planned."

"Does she always give you notice prior to coming here?"

"Usually, but she has dropped by without letting

me know in advance, at least one time."

Detective Powell looked around. "I'm starting to get claustrophobic in here. Close that compartment and set your trap. Then let's go out in the gallery so I can breathe."

Sanders turned to face the cabinet. "Go ahead, detective. I'll be right there."

When Sanders rounded the corner to the main gallery, the detective was mopping his forehead with a handkerchief.

When he saw Sanders, Detective Powell said, "I assume this woman doesn't have a key or know your security code, right?"

Sanders nodded. "That's correct."

The detective gestured toward the rear of the gallery. "Do you have parking out back?"

Sanders wrinkled his forehead. "Yes, there are a couple places back there."

"Good. Now here's my plan. I don't want this woman dropping by unexpectedly. So, you can either agree not to come to your building unless you know she is scheduled to come, or you can park in back and ignore her if she rings the doorbell. In fact, I don't want you to let anyone inside until I say so. We're going to set up a sting for this woman."

He looked at his watch. "I got to run now, but I'll get back with you by the end of the day with our plan."

"Okay, detective."

Detective Powell jerked his head toward the back

wall. "If you're planning to stay here after I leave, I want you to move your car around to the back."

Sanders shook his head. "Give me a minute to pack up my things and I'll leave when you do. I need to get you Sara's card."

The detective nodded.

Sanders set the security alarm and the two men exited the building together.

"Give me a call if you hear from this woman." The detective opened the door to his car.

"Will do."

Sanders spent a few minutes sitting in his Spider before starting it up. He wondered what he was going to do the rest of the day and whether Sara would contact him. Traffic was light on the drive back to his apartment building. He walked into his apartment and flopped down on his sofa.

His phone rang from inside his coat pocket. He fished it out and answered. "Hello."

"Pierce, this is Detective Powell. You have a minute?"

Sanders leaned forward. "Sure, detective."

"You're on speaker. Just so you know, Detective Thurman is here with me. Here's the plan. This is what I want you to do next time this Sara Martin contacts you about coming to your building. If it's the same day, I want you to stall her until the next day. We need the time to set up the operation."

Sanders rubbed his head. "What about if she calls wanting to meet over the weekend?"

Detective Powell sniffed. "Same thing. If she calls you Saturday and wants to stop by Sunday, that's fine. Same day appointments are what we don't want."

"Would you like me to contact her and try to arrange a meeting?"

Detective Powell growled, "Negative. We want her to initiate the meeting. Also, when she arrives at your building, just act normal. Otherwise, she might get spooked. We plan on making the arrest as soon as she exits your building."

"Aren't you worried she might spot you when she arrives?"

"Pierce, this isn't our first rodeo. She won't suspect a thing. Any other questions?"

Sanders sighed. "Yes. Is it possible for me to wear a wire?"

"I considered that, but I don't think it's necessary. We will have her in possession of meth."

"That's why I want to wear a wire. Detective, if I'm correct that the safe on my property has an illegal drug inside, I'm technically in possession. My only defense is that I didn't have knowledge of the possession. If I'm wired, you will hear our conversation and know I'm in no way involved."

The detective chuckled. "Sounds like you have been spending a little time researching this matter on the internet."

Sanders stood up from the sofa. "Detective, I'm an attorney. Admittedly not a criminal law attorney.

Nonetheless, I want to protect myself as much as possible."

Detective Powell groaned. "Okay, Pierce, we'll wire you. Detective Thurman will meet you at your building an hour before this woman is scheduled to arrive. He can wire you and slip out the back door."

"Thank you, detective."

"Any other questions?"

"No, I will contact you as soon as I hear anything from Sara."

"Good, that's the plan. Bye, Pierce."

Chapter 32

Sanders spent a quiet weekend at his apartment. He did not have any contact from either Kat or Sara until Sunday night, when he received a text from Kat confirming their date for the members-only reception Monday at the Dallas Museum of Art. They agreed to meet at 6:45 p.m. just inside the door on the gallery's west side.

At 6:35 p.m. Monday evening, Sanders exited his apartment on foot to make the short trek across Klyde Warren Park to the museum, which was situated on the east side of the park. It was a cool crisp evening. He had decided to dress up a bit from his normal attire and wore gray slacks, a light blue dress shirt with a plaid navy-blue sport coat.

He arrived at the museum on time and found a seat on one of the benches that lined the wall. As he scrolled through email on his cell phone, a familiar voice said, "You look all spiffy tonight."

He glanced up to see Kat standing before him, wearing a black pantsuit and white blouse. Sanders shot to his feet. "Hey there, I didn't see you come in."

She gave him a quick hug. "I'm surprised you haven't already made it over to the bar for a glass of wine."

He smiled. "I was just waiting for you."

They walked over to the bar and drank a quick

glass of wine before entering the gallery which was exhibiting Van Gogh and the Olive Groves series of paintings. After leisurely viewing the exhibition, they left the museum.

"Would you like to go somewhere for a glass of wine?" Sanders said.

Kat motioned with her head. "What about Savor?"

He nodded. "Perfect."

They crossed Klyde Warren Park over to Savor, which was located on the west side. They could see through the ceiling to floor windows that the lounge area was not crowded. Sanders ordered a glass of Simi Chardonnay and Kat a Cakebread Sauvignon Blanc.

"What did you think of the exhibition?" he said.

"Lovely. It was nice to see it with so few other people around."

"That's very true."

The server brought their glasses of wine and set them on the low table in front of them.

Sanders leaned forward and reached to pick up his glass of wine. He paused and then leaned back in his chair. "Kat, I have something I need to talk to you about."

Her eyes narrowed. "This sounds serious. Is something wrong?"

He groaned. "I'm afraid it is serious. Let me start by asking you a direct question. Did your clients really give you those nice pieces of jewelry you have been wearing?"

Kat frowned. "Of course, they did. What are you implying?"

Sanders took a deep breath. "I'm going to be blunt. I know for certain that your clients, Mrs. Davidson and Mrs. Tyler, had severe mental issues. In their condition, they wouldn't have had the mental capacity to intentionally gift you with expensive jewelry. You told me they didn't have mental conditions."

Her mouth dropped open. "You're accusing me of stealing!"

Sanders leaned forward and murmured, "I think it's possible. I so hope it's not true."

Kat hissed. "Do you fancy yourself as some kind of amateur detective?"

He pursed his lips. "No, but it all just doesn't add up. A hospice caregiver cannot possibly make the kind of money required to support your lifestyle. You have a million-dollar home with top-of-the-line furniture and appliances. It's hard to reconcile those luxuries with your salary."

She stood up. "Has it ever occurred to you that perhaps I inherited enough money to support my lifestyle."

He wrinkled his forehead. "But you told me your husband didn't leave you anything."

Kat raised her voice. "He didn't! My dad left me millions, you bastard!"

She stormed out of Savor. Sanders surveyed the restaurant. He sensed everyone was staring at him.

His server approached his table. "Is everything

all right, sir?"

Sanders shook his head. "Far from it. Could I please have the check?"

Chapter 33

Tuesday afternoon, Sanders turned right on Interurban Street from Arapaho Road. One block north of his studio, he took a right on Rayflex Drive and an immediate left into the alley and pulled up behind his building. Sanders parked in the parking space nearest the back door to his building.

He was grateful he remembered to disarm the security system with his phone app before entering the building. Otherwise, he would have had to sprint to the front of the building to enter the security code.

Sanders did not flick on the lights in the main gallery. The gallery space took on an eerie feel in the dark with the heavily tinted windows shielding it from daylight. He went into his studio and turned on a work lamp for light, confident it could not be seen from outside.

He put a new canvas he had recently stretched on the easel and sat staring at it. Nothing came to him. He was void of creativity.

Sanders flipped off his work lamp, plodded over, and crashed on his sofa. All the drama from the evening before kept running through his head.

Was I totally wrong about Kat? Did I just screw up big time?

He closed his eyes and drifted off to sleep. The

front doorbell chime interrupted his nap. Sanders sat up, trying to regain full consciousness. He stumbled out of his studio and over to his office. He squinted at the security monitor.

A thirty-something woman dressed in blue jeans and a white turtleneck sweater was fiddling with the door handle. She pounded on the door several times. The woman gave up after a few seconds and climbed back into the driver's seat of an old Nissan Maxima.

Sanders thought he could detect that she was talking on her cell phone. After about ten minutes, she backed out of the parking space and sped off south on Interurban Street. Once he regained full control of his faculties, he pulled up email on his laptop, half expecting to see an email from Kat continuing to spew venom at him.

Sanders pulled up the dallasnews.com and selected Obituaries. Scrolling through them, his eyes widened when he reached Saturday. The obituary for Harriet Royce was on the second page. He perused it.

The last two lines said, "Harriet was the victim of Alzheimer's Disease. As a result, the family of Mrs. Royce requests in lieu of flowers that a donation be made to The Alzheimer's Research Foundation."

Sanders was now certain his suspicions of Kat were accurate. He shuffled through the top drawer of his desk and pulled out Detective Gonzales' card. Sanders had no contact with the detective since that fateful day when he saved Sanders' life in a tunnel under Maple Street.

He dialed the number on the card. On the third ring, the familiar voice at the other end of the line said, "Detective Gonzales."

"Hello detective, this is Charles Sanders Pierce."

There was a pause at the other end of the line. Sanders assumed Detective Gonzales was trying to recall why his name sounded familiar.

"Pierce, don't tell me you're in trouble again."

"No, detective, I do have an issue I would like to discuss with you, though. Do you have a minute?"

The detective said in a graveled voice, "Shoot."

"I was hoping I could come downtown and talk to you in person."

Detective Gonzales snickered. "Why? Do you miss seeing me? Sure, Pierce, how about 10:00 a.m. tomorrow morning. I'm sure you remember your way to police headquarters."

"Thank you, detective. I'll see you then."

"One last thing Pierce. No one's trying to kill you, are they?"

"No, it's nothing like that. But I do have some information that should be of interest to the Dallas police."

"All right Pierce. I'll see you tomorrow."

"Bye, detective."

Sanders tossed his phone on the desk and leaned back in his chair. The phone chimed right before it hit the desk. He straightened up in his chair and reached for it. There was a text from Sara.

Hey, Sanders, I hope you had a wonderful
weekend. I'm going to be in the mood today
for an exquisite glass of wine. Are you going
to be at your gallery this afternoon? I would
love to stop by and see you. Sara

Sanders pondered the best way to respond.

Hi Sara, I'm not at the gallery today.
I decided to take a few days off. How about
Wednesday afternoon at 4:30 P.M.? I have a
nice chardonnay you'll love. Sanders

Sara confirmed the appointment, and Sanders
contacted Detective Powell to set up the sting operation. Detective Thurman would arrive an hour early
on Wednesday to wire Sanders and prepare the
building. Sanders was to park out front in the middle
parking space.

Detective Powell, Detective Sanders, along with
an officer and K-9, would wait around back until
Sanders texted Detective Powell that Sara had
arrived. When she exited the building, they planned
to make the arrest.

Chapter 34

Wednesday morning at 9:45 a.m., Sanders turned onto S. Lamar Street and parked in the lot adjacent to the Dallas Police Headquarters. He passed through the medical detector and rode the elevator up to the fourth floor.

A young pale thin woman sat at the front desk, staring at her computer screen. Without looking up, she said, "May I help you?"

"Yes, I have an appointment with Detective Gonzales."

The woman picked up a phone. After a long pause, she said, "D3?"

She handed a visitor badge to Sanders. "Room D3, down the hall on your left."

"Thank you." Sanders walked down the hall. It still had the grey-green color paint and linoleum checkered tile. The door was open, so he walked in the room and took the chair opposite the open door.

At 10:15 a.m., Detective Gonzales walked into the room. He was a large husky balding man in his mid-fifties, dressed in a charcoal gray suit, white shirt, and blue tie. "Sorry to keep you waiting, Pierce. I had to put out some fires."

Sanders stood up. "No problem, detective. Thank you for meeting with me."

Detective Gonzales motioned with his hand.

"Have a seat." He slid into the chair opposite Sanders. "What's on your mind?"

Sanders sighed. "I know a woman named Kat Zeman, who I'm certain is stealing from elderly people. She's a hospice caregiver for these poor people. Kat showed up on our dates with expensive jewelry. When I inquired about them, she said they were gifted to her by her clients."

Detective Gonzales eyes narrowed. "What makes you think that they weren't gifts?"

Sanders leaned forward. "Because all these people suffered from Alzheimer's Disease. They didn't have the mental capacity to make a gift of any kind."

The detective rubbed his nose. "And how do you know that."

"In one of the cases, my old college roommate happened to be this person's pastor. In each of the other cases, the obituaries requested that donations be made to various Alzheimer's charities in lieu of flowers." Sanders swallowed. "One woman's obituary didn't mention anything about donations. So, I attended her funeral and learned at the reception that the woman suffered from Alzheimer's Disease."

Detective Gonzales chuckled. "You're a piece of work, Pierce. You're basing your suspicions on obituaries request for donations. Couldn't it be possible that these women's families decided that Alzheimer's charities were worthy causes and that it had nothing to do with the deceased?"

Sanders nodded. "Of course, I thought of that

as well. It's just that I'm aware Kat lied about the woman's condition in the case where I attended the funeral. She said the woman had no mental issues. That was contrary to what the daughter-in-law of the woman told me at the reception."

"How do you know this woman anyway?"

Sanders groaned. "An internet dating website."

The detective rolled his eyes. "How long have you known her?"

"A couple of months. We've had several dates."

"Anything else?"

"Yes, a hospice caregiver in Dallas County makes around fifty thousand dollars a year. Kat's house is worth at least a million dollars with expensive furnishings. No way could she afford that type of house on her salary."

"Did this woman have a husband prior to meeting you? If so, then maybe he left it to her in his will."

Sanders shook his head. "Kat said the only asset he left her was his share of her home in Plano. When I confronted her with my suspicions the other night, she said she inherited money from her dad."

Detective Gonzales shifted in his chair. "And you don't believe her?"

Sanders sighed. "No, she's lied too many times. The latest concerned Harriet Royce, who just passed. After consuming a few drinks one evening, she told me about Mrs. Royce's extensive jewelry collection. I inquired as to why she was in hospice and Kat said she suffered from end stage renal disease. Then I specifically asked if she had any mental issues. She said Mrs. Royce didn't have any mental issues. Her obituary said she had Alzheimer's Disease."

The detective leaned forward and took a pen and small notebook out of his coat pocket. "Okay, Pierce. I know from past experiences with you that you're a little eccentric. But you're also a straight shooter. Give me this woman's full name, address, phone number, place of employment, and everything you can think of that's possibly relevant."

Sanders had gotten up early that morning and prepared the list, anticipating the detective would request this information if he agreed to investigate. He pulled the list out of his coat pocket and flipped it on the table.

Detective Gonzales scanned the list. "You were pretty confident I would look into this matter, weren't you?"

Sanders shook his head. "No, but I wanted to be prepared."

The detective read out loud, "Katherine Zeman. That's an interesting name."

Sanders nodded. "Have you ever read the Dr. Seuss book, *The Cat in the Hat Comes Back*?"

Detective Gonzales wrinkled his forehead. "Why the hell do you ask me that?"

Sanders leaned forward. "It's relevant, I promise."

Detective Gonzales growled. "I'm sure I read it as a kid. Why?"

"I think this woman fancies herself as the Z Cat

character in it."

Detective Gonzales groaned. "I'll take your word for it. Anything else?"

Sanders stood up. "No, detective, thank you for your time."

The detective remained seated. "You know your way out?"

"Yes. Please contact me if you need anything else."

The detective waved his hand over his head without looking around.

Chapter 35

Wednesday afternoon at 3:00 p.m., Sanders arrived at the front of his building. He parked in the middle space as Detective Powell had instructed. It was a mild clear day outside. Sanders chuckled as he thought how Kat would have hated this beautiful weather.

While he waited for Detective Thurman to arrive, he left all the gallery lights turned off with the door locked. Sanders sat in his office, keeping a close eye on the monitor screens projecting the view from the security cameras located in the back and front of his building.

At 3:25 p.m., a dark green Chevrolet Malibu pulled up and parked in one of the spaces at the rear of the building. He recognized Detective Thurman as he got out of his car. The detective carried a black briefcase and waved at the security camera above the door.

Sanders hurried to the back of the building to let the detective inside. He opened the door. "Hello, detective. Come on in."

Detective Thurman nodded. "Mr. Pierce. Lead the way."

Once they were inside the office, the detective rested the briefcase on Sanders' desk and popped it open. As he was rummaging through the briefcase, he said, "What size belt do you wear?"

Sanders reached down and patted his belt. "I have a thirty-four waist. Why do you ask?"

Detective Thurman pulled a belt out of the briefcase. "Because you're gonna be wearing this belt. The buckle contains a body wire transmitter. Here, try it on."

Sanders slipped his belt off and slipped the new belt on. "It fits pretty good. How does it work?"

The detective pointed at the belt. "That buckle will be sending covert monitoring signals to a radio receiver. The surveillance team will be standing by, listening to your conversations."

Sanders reached down and touched the buckle. "Do I need to tuck my shirt in?"

Detective Thurman shook his head. "No, that doesn't make a difference. In fact, it's better if you wear your shirt tail outside. That way the target won't get suspicious."

Sanders said, "It's amazing something so small can broadcast a conversation to another location."

The detective nodded. "That's technology for you. Listen, I want to place another device somewhere in the restroom, in case she has a phone call with someone."

Sanders gestured toward the rear of the building. "Let's go on back. We got about forty-five minutes before Sara is due to arrive."

The detective entered the guest restroom, flipped on the lights, and searched for the right location to place a listening device. He reached behind the toilet lid. "Perfect. There's just enough room."

The detective removed a strip from the bottom of the device and placed it on the wall behind the toilet. It was not visible from anywhere in the restroom. "That should do it. Let me get my briefcase and I'll be out of here."

Sanders waited by the back door for the detective to retrieve his briefcase.

Detective Thurman reappeared. "Any questions before I go."

Sanders shook his head. "No, I can't think of any."

The detective glanced at his wristwatch. "In ten minutes at 4:10 p.m., I want you to talk in your normal voice so we can make sure your belt transmitter is live. These devices are pretty reliable, so I don't anticipate any problems. We will text you if all is a go."

Sanders opened the door. "Will do, detective."

He locked the door behind Detective Thurman and walked to the front of the gallery. Sanders then switched on the gallery lights and selected a station on Pandora to create a scene of normalcy. Satisfied, he retreated to his office to wait for Sara. The time on his computer screen indicated it was 4:07 p.m.

A precise three minutes later, Sanders spoke. "Just testing. It's a nice day outside. I certainly hope everything goes as planned." He stood up and walked to the door to his office. "Just testing a different location. It's a nice—"

The phone in his coat pocket chimed. He whipped it out. A text from Detective Powell specified the transmitter was functioning properly.

Sanders slumped back into his chair and stared at the monitor screen. He had flipped off the monitor for the rear security cameras as an added precaution.

Now, where's Sara?

At 4:40 p.m., a black BMW Z4 pulled in front of the building and parked in the space nearest the front door. Sara got out of the driver's seat. She opened the trunk and removed a large bag. Sanders recognized it as the bag she often carried when she visited the gallery.

Sanders texted Detective Powell that Sara had arrived at the building. She wore a beige sport coat, light blue shirt, and blue jeans. Sara walked over to the door and attempted to open it, but the door was locked. She spun around and waved at the security camera above.

Sanders switched on the intercom. "I'll be right there, Sara."

She waved again and waited by the door.

Sanders felt a pit in his stomach as he trudged to the front of the gallery. He hated having to be part of the effort to arrest her, although he knew she was likely deserving of it.

He took a deep breath to calm his nerves before unlocking the door. He opened it and smiled at Sara.

"What took you so long?" she said with a grin. "Feels like I've been out front for hours."

He stood aside for her to come inside. "Sorry, I was in my office finishing up some business."

Sara walked over and plopped her bag down on top of the bar.

Sanders followed her. "Would you like a glass of wine?"

She hopped up on the stool next to her purse. "Of course. But first I want a hug."

Sara gave him a tight hug. Her body pressed up against his belt buckle. He wondered whether she could feel it. She gazed up at him. "What excellent wine are you serving today?"

"Rombauer Chardonnay."

Her eyes widened. "Wonderful."

Sara hopped up on the stool nearest her bag and Sanders opened the refrigerator and pulled out a bottle of Rombauer Chardonnay. He opened it earlier so he wouldn't have to fumble with popping the cork in front of her.

Sanders poured two glasses and returned the wine bottle to the refrigerator. He remained standing behind the bar right across from Sara.

Sara gave him a friendly smile. "What creative project are you working on in your studio?"

He grimaced. "I've been taking some time off lately." He did not want to prolong Sara's visit.

"Well, then what have you been up to?"

He took a sip of chardonnay. "Not too much really. I had a meeting with my investment advisor. That's pretty much all the excitement in my life."

Sara eyes narrowed. "By the way, how's my competition these days. What's her name again?"

Sanders snickered. "Kat, and she's doing fine."

"Have you been out on a date recently?"

He nodded. "We went to an art event last Monday night. But that's it."

She flipped her blond hair. "That's doesn't sound too romantic."

He smiled. "It wasn't."

Sara took a gulp of wine. "Sounds like you didn't enjoy it. Are you seeing her this weekend?"

"No. We didn't make any plans."

She reached across the bar and patted his hand. "Why don't we go to dinner Saturday?"

He took a sip of wine. "Did you have anything in mind?"

"We could meet here and then go up to Jaspers."

He nodded. "Sounds good."

"Great, we have a date." She finished her glass of wine. "I need to go powder my nose."

Sanders motioned with his head. "You know where the restroom is located."

She stood up and grabbed her bag. "I'll be back in a jiff."

Sanders walked around the bar and scooted onto the bar stool at the far end. He cast a quick glance over his shoulder at the front of the gallery. He suspected the detectives were waiting out front.

Sara returned about ten minutes later.

Sanders said, "Would you like a refill?"

She shook her head. "Thank you, but no. I really need to be going."

Sanders stood up and gave her hug. Once he released her, she hurried toward the front of the gallery her heels clicking on the floor. She shouted, "Remember our date Saturday!"

He didn't respond but held up his empty wine glass and pretended to toast her. When the door closed behind her, Sanders sprinted to his office monitor and got there just in time to see Detective Thurman placing handcuffs on Sara. He watched as a uniformed officer put her in the back seat of a Richardson Police SUV. Her face was streaked with tears.

What a pity!

The front door buzzed as it was opened. Sanders rushed to the gallery. Detective Powell stood just inside the gallery. When he spotted Sanders, he said, "It's done."

Sanders was out of breath. "Did she have the meth?"

The detective nodded. "All can I say with a hundred percent certainty is that she had a dozen little film cases full of some kind of substance that sure appear to be meth. The lab will have to confirm, but Charlie was damn certain."

Sanders furrowed his brow. "Charlie?"

Detective Powell chuckled. "You remember our four-legged, K-9 sniffing officer?"

Sanders smiled. "Of course. Now I do. What's next?"

He gestured toward the back of the gallery. "We need to get into that safe sooner than later."

"Can't you get Sara to open it?"

The detective shook his head. "The woman's playing ignorant. She claims she had no idea how the meth ended up in her bag."

Sanders said, "I can call John Shapiro and tell him that it's now a police matter."

"Do that and see if he can come tonight."

Sanders pulled his phone out of his pocket and dialed the expert safe cracker.

John answered on the second ring. "Shapiro, here."

Sanders put his phone on speaker so that Detective Powell could hear the conversation. "Mr. Shapiro, this is Sanders Pierce."

"Yes, the man with the mysterious safe. You ready to set a date to open it?"

"Yes, I'm standing here next to Richardson Detective Powell, so the matter has become more urgent. Is there any way we could schedule it tonight?"

There was a pause at the other end of the line. "To be honest, I was hoping to watch the Cowboys game on TV tonight."

The detective grunted, "This is Detective Powell. We have a safe here that could be holding a boatload of illegal drugs and we need the damn thing opened tonight. Will you help us?"

"Uh, sure detective, no problem. I can be there no

later than 8:00 p.m."

"Perfect, we'll be waiting for you."

After the phone call, Detective Powell said, "You run on and get some dinner. I'll do the same and then we'll meet back here at 7:30 p.m."

"Okay, detective."

The detective motioned with his head. "I'll step out front and wait for you while you set the security alarm."

Sanders armed the security system and locked the door to the building.

Detective Powell said, "I'll have squad cars parked out front and back until we return tonight."

AT 7:20 P.M., DETECTIVE POWELL was sitting in his car in front of the building. When Sanders pulled the Spider in the space next to him, the detective exited his car.

A squad car inched forward, heading north on Interurban Street. Detective Powell waved at it. "Let's hope this doesn't turn out to be a waste of time."

Sanders unlocked the door and disarmed the security system. The two men went inside. Sanders took a seat at the bar and the detective slid into a chair under one of the paintings in the gallery. At 8:05 p.m., car lights flickered through the tinted windows.

Sanders walked over and opened the door. John Shapiro was parked in the space nearest the front door. He appeared to be engaged in a call on his phone. He nodded toward him and Sanders assumed he was letting him know he would be finished soon.

John slipped the phone in his coat pocket, got out of his Porsche SUV, and grabbed a backpack from the back seat. The same as before, he was dressed in a sport coat, crisp white shirt, blue jeans, and cowboy boots. "The Cowboys are down by a touchdown."

Sanders frowned. "I'm sorry we had to interfere with the game."

"No worries."

Sanders introduced John to Detective Powell and the three men made their way back to the restroom. Sanders flipped on the light and opened the mirror cabinet. John set his pack down on the closed commode seat. He looked around at them. "Would you gentleman mind waiting in the hall. I need space and quiet to do my work."

Detective Powell said, "What kind of technique do you use?"

As John was pulling out some tools out of his pack, he said, "Borescope. I drill a miniscule hole through the door and insert the borescope to get an intimate look at the security container."

He might as well be speaking in French as far as Sanders was concerned.

Detective Powell said, "So you're drilling the lock?"

John snickered. "Not exactly. That's like comparing setting a broken bone to brain surgery."

The detective said, "All right, we'll get out of your

hair so you can work."

John turned around to face the cabinet. "Much obliged."

The men stepped back into the main gallery. A high-pitched shrill noise came from the direction of the restroom.

The detective said, "That must be the drill."

Twenty minutes later, John emerged from around the corner. "It's showtime, gentlemen."

The three men returned to the restroom. A very thin wire poked through a hole next to the safe's keypad. John walked over to the safe and tapped the digits one, three, five, seven, nine on the keypad. The door opened and a small bulb just inside on the left lit up red.

John pointed at the light, "Whoever installed this safe knows it's been breached."

Detective Powell took his cell phone out of his coat pocket and turned on the flashlight app. Small canvas bags were stacked on the left side and dozens of film roll containers on the right side. He pointed his light at them. "That's the same kind of containers that woman was carrying in her bag."

John said, "What do you think is in them?"

The detective said, "My guess is that each one contains meth." He pulled a pair of plastic gloves out of his pocket and slipped them on, then reached inside and removed one of the containers and popped it open. "Yep, pretty sure."

Sanders scratched his head. "Why did they keep

their meth here? That seems so risky."

"Actually, it's pretty ingenious," Detective Powell said. "The kingpin can't be charged with possession. All that's required is to have an inside contact who has access to the safe without raising your suspicion. I'm assuming that young woman is that person."

Sanders nodded. "You're probably right. Her initial cover was that she was a P.R. person who could help in promoting my opening. When that was over, she pretended to be romantically interested in me. It almost worked. Also, the tenants who leased this building before I purchased it were supposedly photographers. Now I suspect that was a cover for their meth lab."

Detective Powell said, "That would also explain the strange plumbing in here."

John stuck his penlight inside the safe. "Look in the back behind the containers. That looks like a small camera mounted to the back wall. Somebody's probably looking at us right now."

Sanders narrowed his eyes. "Sara wasn't the only one who accessed the safe. Maybe that explains how the kingpin monitored what was deposited and removed from the safe."

Detective Powell said, "A forensics team is on alert to come and remove all the contents. I'm gonna contact them, now we got the safe open."

John packed up his tools and the men walked around the corner into the main gallery space.

John said, "Mr. Pierce, I'll email you an invoice in

the morning."

"Thanks John. I appreciate you coming out tonight."

He smiled as he said, "If I hurry, I might be able to catch part of the fourth quarter." Right before he reached the front door, he whirled around. "Better watch your back, Mr. Pierce."

Sanders groaned. "Thanks. I will."

The forensics team consisted of two men and a woman, who fingerprinted and removed all the contents of the safe, and then placed them in large evidence bags and labeled them.

It was near midnight before they finished their work. After they left, Detective Powell said, "Quite an evening. Shall we go?"

Sanders sighed, "Yes, I'm beat."

The detective gestured toward the front door. "I'll wait outside while you set the security alarm."

Sanders armed the system and locked the door behind him. "Detective, what happens next?"

"We hope the woman cracks and gives us some names of those involved. In the meantime, you better be careful."

A chill shot down Sanders' spine. "I will, detective."

The detective opened his car door. "I'll be in touch to keep you updated."

"Thank you."

Sanders slept well Wednesday night. He decided he wouldn't return to his building until Monday. He wanted a little bit of normality in his life. It was a bit strange though, not receiving any texts or emails from either Kat or Sara. Two people who were part of his life were now history.

I hope Sara decides to cooperate!

Chapter 36

Monday was a beautiful cool November day in Dallas. Sanders was invigorated after a restful weekend binging on football games on TV and strolls on the Katy Trail. He looked forward to a productive day painting in his studio.

An idea for a new painting had come to him while he was out walking on Sunday. Sanders spotted two young women wearing what appeared to him as two identical little black dresses. Was it accidental or purposeful, that they wore the same outfit? Regardless, he decided to paint an abstract painting entitled *Little Black Dress*. It was rare for him to name a painting before he even started it.

Sanders arrived at his building and spent almost an hour stretching a new canvas. Satisfied it was properly stretched, he squeezed out a healthy portion of black paint from a tube onto a palette, followed by a similar amount of medium. He mixed the two together until the paint spread very smoothly. Sanders covered the entire canvas in black paint. He anticipated that black would constitute the background color, with very little showing, once he was finished with the painting.

Sanders cleaned his brush and palette before retiring to his office to wait for the background to dry. He sat down at his desk and by habit glanced up at the security monitor screen for the front camera. It was pitch black. The rear camera appeared to be operating properly. Sanders checked to make sure the front monitor had power.

Damn, that camera must be on the blink.

He spent the next thirty minutes searching for someone who repairs external security cameras. Sanders at last found a local company who performed this type of service and he booked an appointment for Wednesday.

He went back into the studio and spent the next two tedious hours painting long narrow lines which resembled strips of wood. The black background served as the spacing between each strip. Sanders leaned back in his chair. He was pleased with the day's work and decided to call it a day.

After cleaning and straightening his studio, he strolled through the gallery, admiring the work hanging on the walls. Sanders armed the security alarm and locked the door. His Spider was parked in the usual middle space. He unlocked the door and slid into the driver's seat.

Sanders turned on the ignition, expecting to hear the Miles Davis station on Pandora. Nothing but the sound of the Spider's motor idling. He patted his coat pocket for his phone. Nothing was there.

Shoot! I must have left my phone in the office.

Sanders switched off the ignition and hurried back into his building. He entered his office and spied his phone on his desk next to his computer keyboard. Sanders grabbed it and headed back through the gallery to the front. He armed the security system again and pulled on the handle to open the front door.

The door blew off its hinges inside the gallery. Sanders was knocked down on the concrete floor and the door landed on top of him. Everything went black.

When he opened his eyes, blurry images hovered over him. His ears were ringing. At last Sanders eyes could focus.

Two firemen knelt on either side of his prone body. The one to his right said, "Are you okay?"

"He probably has a concussion," the other one said.

Sanders shifted his head a bit to the left. The entire front tinted windows were gone. Shards of broken glass lay next to him on the concrete floor. "What happened?"

The fireman on his right said, "Some type of explosion. You're lucky to be alive."

Sanders sat up. "Is my car... okay?"

The firemen glanced at one another. The one on the right said, "Sir, your car is a crumbled heap of metal, rubber, and glass. We suspect it was ground zero for the explosion."

A familiar voice said, "How's he doing?" Detective Powell stood in what used to be the threshold of the front door.

The fireman on the right said, "He's a bit dinged up."

Detective Powell approached them. "Sorry about this, Pierce."

Sanders nodded toward the chair next to the wall.

"Can you help me over there?"

The firemen grabbed Sanders under both arms and helped him stagger over to a chair and sit down.

Detective Powell said, "I do have some good news."

Sanders rubbed the back of his head. He could feel a tender spot where his head hit the concrete floor. "As you might imagine, detective, I can use some good news."

The detective rubbed his nose. "Your lady friend cracked. She's now cooperating with us. We know the identity of the kingpin and have an A.P.B. out for him and his henchmen."

Sanders said, "I assume he's responsible for this mayhem."

Detective Powell nodded. "I have no doubt. They were out to get revenge on someone, and you were the obvious soft target. Can you tell me what you remember right before the explosion?"

Sanders sighed, "Yes, I was through painting for the day. I started my Spider and then remembered I had left my phone in the office. So, I turned the car off and went back inside to get my phone. I alarmed the security alarm and was about to open the door when I blacked out."

Detective Powell said, "I suspect they planted a bomb under your car which was timed to explode five minutes after you started the ignition. You're damn lucky you forgot your phone, or we would not be having this conversation."

Sanders nodded. "My car was not so lucky."

The detective drew closer. "Do you think you can walk?"

"Yes, I'm much better."

Detective Powell put one hand under Sanders' left arm and helped him to his feet. "I'll give you a ride home."

Sanders pointed at the opening where the tinted glass windows once inhabited the frame. "What about that gaping hole in my building?"

"I already spoke with your next-door neighbor, and he has some plywood and volunteered to cover the openings."

Sanders fell asleep on the ride back to his apartment and woke up when the detective pulled into the driveway. He did not remember how he got up to his apartment but was relieved to be lying down on his sofa in the living room.

Chapter 37

Sanders cocooned in his apartment all day Tuesday. He spent the better part of the day dealing with different aspects of the explosion, including applying an ice pack on the back of his head. The last item on his agenda was getting a rental car until he could get a settlement check from his insurance company.

The company arranged to have a Subaru SUV delivered to his apartment building. The valet parked it in the garage and brought the keys up to his apartment.

Sanders went to bed early and slept ten hours. He woke up at 8:30 a.m. to the sound of thunder. Rain pounded against the bedroom window. Sanders got out of bed, showered, and devoured some scrambled eggs and toast.

He felt a calm he had not experienced in a while. The drama of Sara and the mysterious safe were now in the rear-view mirror. Sanders could focus on the future and restoring his building. He put on his runners, grabbed an umbrella, and headed out to Klyde Warren Park. It was completely vacant.

His cell phone rang. Sanders fished it out of the pocket of his sweatpants and glanced at it to see who was calling. Kat Z. was illuminated on the screen. He jogged to get under an overhang of Savor Restaurant to escape the rain. "Hello."

The recognizable voice on the other end of the line

said, "Thank God, you picked up."

"Kat? You sound a little distraught."

"I'm very distraught. Are you at your apartment?"

"No, I'm in Klyde Warren Park. What's wrong?"

"Can I please come over?"

"Now?"

"Yes, it's very important. I'm afraid to go home."

"Why are you afraid to go home?"

"I'll explain. May I please come over now?"

"Yes. I'll be home in about ten minutes."

"Thank you, Sanders." Kat hung up.

Sanders dropped the phone back into his sweat-pants pocket.

What the hell's going on with her? She hates my guts!

As Sanders made his way back to his apartment, all types of scenarios played out in his head as to what this whole business might be about. He showered in a hurry and changed into blue jeans and a sweatshirt.

Because it's raining, I thought Kat would be ecstatic and not afraid to go home. That's crazy. Why the hell is she coming here?

AT 1:00 P.M., SANDERS' PHONE rang on the kitchen counter. He raced across the room and answered it. "Hello."

"Mr. Pierce, this is Carol at the concierge desk. A Ms. Zeman is here to see you. Shall I send her up?"

He sighed. "Yes, please."

A few minutes passed before a soft knock came at the door. Sanders peered through the peep hole. Seeming nervous, Kat looked back and forth down the hall outside. He opened the door and she rushed inside. She was dressed in blue jeans, runners, and a red pullover sweater. Her strawberry blond hair was pulled back in a ponytail.

Kat gave Sanders a tight hug. "Thank you for letting me come over." She gazed up at him. Her face was drawn, and her eyes were bloodshot.

He motioned toward the sofa. "Would you like to sit down?"

Without answering, Kat walked over and sat down on the sofa.

Sanders set down next to her. "What's going on?"

She took a deep breath. "Some man is stalking me."

Sanders eyes widened. "Really? Are you sure?"

Kat nodded. "I'm positive. A couple of days ago was the first time I became suspicious. I was in the grocery store. Everywhere I went in the store, I kept crossing paths with this sleazy-looking guy. When I tried to make eye contact, he turned his head and looked away."

She shrugged. "I didn't think much of it until I was driving home. A car trailed behind me, making every turn I made. I took a circuitous way home on purpose and he stayed on my tail. As you know, I live on the corner. I pulled into the alley behind my house and hit the remote control to open the gate to my driveway. The car tailing me sat idling in the street at the entrance to the alley. A man inside it stared at me. I pulled my car into the driveway and kept an eye on my rear-view mirror until my gate closed behind me."

Sanders shifted his weight on the sofa. "Did he try to follow you into your driveway?"

"No, thank God."

"Maybe it was just some creep with nothing better to do than follow you."

Kat rubbed her eyes. "That's what I thought at first. But later that afternoon, I walked out to the mailbox to check on my mail. You know that two story, white ultra-contemporary house under construction a couple of houses north on the street that intersects mine?"

Sanders nodded. "Yes. I'm familiar with it."

"As I was getting my mail out of the box, I glanced down the street and saw the same car parked in front of that house."

His eyes narrowed. "Are you sure it was the same car?"

She sniffed. "Yes. I think he parked there so he could monitor my whereabouts, whether I came out of the front of my house or the rear alley."

"That's certainly possible. You said this happened a couple of days ago. Have you seen him since then?"

Kat shook her head. "No."

Sanders rubbed his head. "Well, maybe that's the

end of it."

She sighed. "I don't think so. I was put on administrative leave by my supervisor, Mrs. Singleton, first thing this morning."

He cocked his head. "I'm sorry to hear that, but I fail to see the connection."

"My supervisor said she was not at liberty to say why, but told me I would not be able provide hospice care while they dealt with an internal investigation."

"Did she share the nature of this investigation?"

Kat shook her head. "No, she wouldn't say anything. I can assure you I haven't done anything wrong. I'm friends with the receptionist. When I left my supervisor's office, I stopped by her desk and asked if she knew why I was placed on administrative leave. She looked around to make sure no one was looking and whispered, 'Some man came in and met with Mrs. Singleton. When he was leaving her office, I overheard Mrs. Singleton say that she wouldn't tell Kat why she was being put on administrative leave.' That's how I found out."

Sanders leaned in. "And you think this is the same man who was following you?"

"Yes, I do, and I'm scared this guy is after me."

"Why don't you call the police?"

She sobbed. "No. I'm a nervous wreck. Can I stay here, just for a while?"

Sanders leaned back. "Kat, why did you really call me? After our last date, I thought you hated my guts. Then today, you ask me if you can stay with me while supposedly some stalker is out to get you."

The intensity of Kat's sobs increased. "I'm sorry. You hurt my feelings when you accused me of stealing from my clients. I only do hospice work because I love helping people through the most difficult times of their lives. Believe me, I have plenty of money. I don't need to work. I'm a good person."

He patted Kat's arm. "I'm sincerely sorry for your problems. But you can't stay here. If I were you and I thought some guy was stalking me, I would call the police."

Kat sprung to her feet. "I was right the other night. You're a bastard." She stormed over to the door and slammed it shut behind her.

Sanders remained sitting on the couch. He rubbed his head.

Is she scamming me or is there some kernel of truth here?

IN THE AFTERNOON, Sanders decided to drive up and check on his building. He parked his rental Subaru in the space next to the one his Spider used to occupy. Charred marks from the explosion stained several yards of pavement in the parking lot in front of the building.

Sanders inspected the plywood covering the door opening and the missing windows. His neighbor had done a stellar job installing the temporary façade.

Sanders' phone rang from inside his coat pocket.

He fished it out and answered it on the third ring. "Hello, Detective Gonzales."

"Hello, Pierce. Do you have a few minutes?"

"Yes, I'm just checking what's left of the front of my building."

There was a pause at the other end of the line. "What happened to your building?"

Sanders leaned against the hood of the Subaru. "Someone put an explosive under my car intended for me. Long story short, I escaped harm except for a knot on the back of my head. However, my car was destroyed and my building damaged."

"I saw an article in the paper about that. That's in Richardson, isn't it?"

Sanders sighed. "Believe it or not, I was working with the Richardson police on a sting at my gallery. A detective here speculates it was a revenge bombing."

Detective Gonzales chuckled. "Oh, I believe you, Pierce. You seem to be a magnet for trouble. Anyway, I'm sorry to hear about the explosion and I'm glad you survived it. I do have some news for you though. We arrested this Miss Seuss lady an hour ago."

Sanders eyes widened. "So, you confirmed she was stealing from her clients?"

"You don't know the whole story on this lady. She's a bad character. To your question, we know she stole from Harriet Royce. We're also preparing to charge her with manslaughter."

"Did you say manslaughter?"

"Yes, we got lucky with this one. Harriet Royce

was cremated. In Texas, an autopsy is automatically performed under these circumstances. The coroner found a significant quantity of GHB, which is short for gamma hydroxybutyric in her system. He determined it to be a contributing cause of Royce's death. When she was taken into custody, this Kat had vials in her purse that forensics are testing for GHB."

Sanders scratched his head. "What's GHB anyway?"

"It's a depressant that's commonly referred to as a date rape drug."

Sanders' mouth dropped open. "Oh, my God. I never would have guessed Kat was capable of doing something like that. She called me this morning, all distraught that some man was stalking her."

"That was one of our detectives keeping surveillance of her whereabouts. What did she want from you?"

"She asked if she could stay with me for a while."

Detective Gonzales laughed. "How did that play out?"

"I said no and sent her on her way. My response was not well received."

"I'm sure it wasn't."

"Thank you for updating me, detective."

"You're welcome, Pierce. By the way, you may be called to testify if this thing goes to trial."

Sanders heaved a deep sigh. "I understand, detective. Goodbye."

Kat Z. is history!

Chapter 38

Thursday afternoon, Sanders' cell phone rang on the coffee table in his apartment. He picked it up. "Hello."

"Mr. Pierce, this is Carol from the concierge desk. You have received a package. Would you like to have it sent up?"

"Yes, please."

Ten minutes later, a knock came at his door.

Sanders peered through the peep hole. A young man he recognized as one of the valets stood outside the door, holding a package. He opened the door, thanked the valet, and deposited the package on the kitchen counter.

Sanders hunted through his silverware drawer for a steak knife to cut the tape from the box. He pried the lid off with a knife and stared in disbelief at the contents.

Inside was a hardbound copy of *The Cat in the Hat Comes Back*. Sanders removed it and retired to his sofa. He opened the book and flipped through the pages. A chill shot down his spine when he came to page 59.

On the left side of the page was an animated VOOM and in the middle of the word was glued a picture of a black FIAT spider identical to his demolished car. On the right side of the page circled in red ink were text from the book, "Then the VOOM, It went VOOM, And, oh boy, what a VOOM!"

Sanders picked up the phone and dialed Detective Gonzales.

After two rings, the familiar gruff voice said, "Detective Gonzales."

"Detective, this is Sanders Pierce. I think we've got a new wrinkle to the Kat Zeman case."

"What's that?"

"A box was delivered to me today which contained a hardbound copy of *The Cat in the Hat Comes Back*. On page 59 inside was a picture of a black FIAT Spider pasted onto the word VOOM and circled on the right side of the page were the words Then the VOOM, It went VOOM, And, oh boy, what a VOOM."

Detective Gonzales cleared his throat. "I think you lost me, Pierce."

Sanders stood up. "VOOM is a word Kat always used in emails and texts from the book. VOOM is where the Z Cat blows up all the pink off the snow. I drove a car that was identical to the one pasted in the book, and it was blown up in front of my building."

"I understand the connection now. Didn't you tell me that you were working with a detective in the Richardson Police Department?"

"Yes, Detective Powell."

"We have a cross jurisdiction matter on our hands. You call Detective Powell and see if you can arrange a meeting for the three of us. Tell him I'll come to the Richardson headquarters."

"Will do. Thank you, detective."

FRIDAY AFTERNOON, SANDERS pulled into the parking lot of the brand-new Richardson Police Headquarters located at the intersection of Greenville Avenue and Main Street. He had driven by the building numerous times while it was under construction but had never been inside. As Sanders was making his way up to the front door, he spotted Detective Gonzales standing at the top of the steps.

The detective was on his cell phone and nodded at Sanders. He finished his phone call and said, "Swanky building for a police headquarters."

Sanders smirked, "Are you jealous, detective?"

Detective Gonzales chuckled. "Perhaps. Let's go inside."

The men went inside, and Detective Gonzales flashed his badge at the officer operating the security metal detectors. The officer motioned with his head to the left. "You don't have to go through it, detective."

The detective nodded and step around the metal detector.

Sanders went through the metal detector and Detective Gonzales waited for him on the other side. They checked in with reception and within a few minutes Detective Powell greeted them. He led them to a small conference room.

Detective Powell said, "I like to start by thanking you both for agreeing to meet here. I'm up to my neck in paperwork."

"No problem," Detective Gonzales said. "I know

how that is."

Detective Powell said, "Since the explosion occurred in Richardson then, I assume with your cooperation, of course, that Richardson will take the lead on this aspect of the investigation. I know from what Pierce has told me, this Kat Zeman is involved with other criminal matters that were perpetrated in Dallas.

Detective Gonzales said, "That's protocol. You will have our full cooperation with the explosion investigation."

"I don't know if this is the appropriate moment," Sanders said, "but I've been thinking a lot about this matter and I have theory of who's behind the explosion."

Detective Powell gestured with his right hand. "Go for it."

Sanders leaned in and rested his elbows on the table. "I think the whole book thing was a distraction to make us think it was Kat who was involved with the explosion. Yes, she did often quote from the book, especially the whole VOOM thing. But I think it was the drug dealers who did the deed."

Detective Gonzales shifted in his chair. "How would they know about the whole Cat in the Hat fixation this woman had?"

"Through Sara, or whatever her real name is. Sara had feigned a romantic interest in me. "

Detective Powell said, "We got her to tell us her real name is Claudia Moore."

Sanders continued. "When Claudia learned I was dating Kat, she wanted to know everything about her supposed competition. I specifically remembered telling her about how Kat liked the whole Cat in the Hat thing and often ended her emails and texts with VOOM. It's likely she passed this information on to her boss, who came up with the idea to send me the book."

Detective Powell said, "I assume this Claudia knew where you lived?"

Sanders nodded. "Yes, she had been to my apartment."

"That's certainly a plausible theory," Detective Powell said. "A bombing is more up the alley of these drug dealer types."

"When Sanders first contacted me about the book and possible connection to Kat," Detective Gonzales said, "I just couldn't picture her doing that. But you never know with these criminals. She certainly was capable of killing."

Detective Powell looked at the other detective. "Does she have a lawyer?"

Detective Gonzales nodded. "Yep. She's not talking. We have a warrant to search her home on Monday. You're welcome to have someone from Richardson there."

"Thank you, Detective Gonzales. I'll take you up on that. Anybody got anything else?"

"Detective Powell," Sanders said, "have you made any arrests other than Claudia related to the meth?"

"Yes, we've arrested two guys who work for Vince Barone. This Barone is the Meth kingpin. We'll get him soon enough."

After the meeting, Sanders drove west on Main Street and took a right on Interurban Street. He drove down the alley and parked behind his building. Sanders had not gone back inside since the explosion. He unlocked the back door and relocked it behind him.

Sanders walked to the front to survey the damage. It appeared that most of the destruction was limited to the windows and front door. The old building had been built like a fortress. None of the paintings in the gallery was damaged from the explosion.

He went into his office and plopped down into his desk chair. Sanders glanced up at the security monitor for the front door. He had forgotten about the appointment he had made to have it repaired.

Someone probably disabled the camera so I wouldn't see whoever it was that placed the bomb under the Spider.

The monitor for the back door security camera was still functioning the way it should. Sanders watched as a car backed into the space next to the rental Subaru SUV and parked.

A man dressed in a black leather coat, black slacks, white shirt, and dark sunglasses got out of the driver's seat. As he ambled up to the back door, his head twisted back and forth, scanning the surrounding area. He banged on the metal back door and waved at the security camera.

Sanders switched on the intercom. "Can I help you?"

The man said, "I'm Richardson Police Detective Watson." He pulled out of his coat what resembled a police officer's badge. "Here's my badge."

Sanders pretended the camera was not operative. He hoped the man would let his guard down if he thought Sanders could not see him. "I'm sorry, my back camera is malfunctioning. I can't see anything. Why are you here?"

The man slipped the badge back into his pocket. "I'm doing some follow up investigation on the explosion."

Sanders leaned back in his chair. "I was just in the Richardson Police Headquarters meeting with a detective about the explosion. He didn't mention that any follow up was needed."

The man paced a few steps as he pounded his fist into his palm. "Listen, man, I'm just trying to do my job. May I please come inside? I can show you my badge as soon as you open the door."

Sanders stared at the monitor. "Give me a few minutes and I'll be right there."

"Okay, man."

Sanders continued to watch the screen. The man reached into his coat pocket and pulled out a pistol.

Sanders picked up his phone and dialed the number of Detective Powell. It went straight into voice mail. Sanders left a message about the man at the rear door to his building and then walked to the back of the gallery and down the hallway to his broom closet.

He reached in the closet and pulled out a thirty-six-inch Louisville Slugger baseball bat, a gift from Rachel Holbrook, a friend of his who manages a wine bar in Dallas. She always kept a similar bat under the bar in case of trouble.

When she learned Sanders was opening an art gallery, she had showed up one afternoon with the bat wrapped in a ribbon. Sanders was now grateful to have received the gift.

He crept up to the huge rear door and stood on the right side of the threshold, opposite the hinges. When opening, the door would swing inwards. Sanders turned the bolt upwards, unlocking the door, and waited with the bat held with both hands over his head.

"The door's unlocked."

Inch by inch the door opened, and the man took a step inside. He held the pistol drawn in his right hand. As soon as Sanders spotted the pistol, he slammed the bat down with all the force he could muster. The pistol dropped, clanking on the concrete floor. The man doubled up and screamed in pain.

Sanders swung the bat again and landed a blow to the back of the man's head. His body crumpled to the floor face down. He was motionless.

Sanders kicked the pistol across the room. He was trembling but managed to call 9-1-1. Sanders stood guard over the man's body as he waited for the police. Three minutes later, two uniformed officers and Detective Powell appeared at the open back door.

The man on the ground made gurgling sounds. One officer slipped a pair of handcuffs on him. The officers rolled him over, so he lay face up.

Detective Powell said, "Looks like you got Vince Barone singlehanded. Good work, Pierce."

Sanders leaned the bat up against the wall. "I tried to call you, detective."

The detective nodded. "I got your message. That's why I'm here."

Sanders studied the face of the man he had cold-cocked. "I've seen this man before. He attended my opening. I thought then he was sizing up the place and me."

Detective Powell snickered. "Looks like you sized him up also."

Chapter 39

It was an unseasonably warm clear day in February. Sanders eased his new black FIAT Spider into the parking lot in front of his building. He got out of his car and stood admiring the new clear plate glass windows that adorned the front of his building.

Sanders glanced up at the security camera and shook his head. He had procrastinated getting the camera repaired. The gallery took on a completely different look during the day with the clear windows in front. The interior of the gallery was sunbathed with light.

Sanders spent all afternoon painting in his studio. It was a creative and fulfilling day. He cleaned up and grabbed his wallet and car keys from his office and almost trotted to the front of the gallery. Sanders armed the alarm, locked the door, and spun around.

He felt a chill and his mouth dropped open. Scribbled in pink chalk on the concrete next to his Spider in ten-inch letter was the word VOOM. Sanders walked over to where the word was scribbled and stared down at the letters.

This can't be happening!

From the south side of his parking lot, a woman said, "I'm sorry, sir."

Sanders whipped his head around in the direction of the voice. A young woman held the hand of small six- to seven-year-old boy. Tears had welled up in the boy's eyes. He clutched the remnants of pink chalk in his right hand.

The woman said, "My son wants to apologize for messing up your parking lot."

Sanders smiled. "That's quite all right."

She said, "Johnny's just learn how to read and his favorite book is—"

"*The Cat in the Hat Comes Back*." Sanders grinned at them.

Her eyes widened. "That's correct."

Sanders walked over to them. "That's a wonderful book. I bet Johnny's favorite character is Z Cat."

The little boy smiled and nodded.

"Johnny, you're a talented young artist," Sanders said. "I should know because I'm an artist, too."

The woman said, "Thank you, sir for understanding."

Sanders patted the young boy's head. "Enjoy this beautiful day."

ABOUT THE AUTHOR

Jim Lively is currently the Artist and Curator at Martsolf Lively Contemporary in Richardson, Texas. After practicing law for many years, Jim decided to pursue his passion full time as a visual artist, film maker, and author. He received the 2016 Merrimack Media Outstanding Writer Award for his second novel, ***Punitive Damages***. ***Choking on the Splinters*** is the third

novel in a trilogy. ***Surreal Absurdity***, a Global Book Bronze Award winner is a sequel to his novel, ***Aberrant Behavior***.

His artwork and art films have been recognized in numerous juried competitions, publications and film festivals. He has exhibited his artwork in several group and solo exhibitions across North America and Europe.

Fourteen of Jim's films have been selected to various film festivals around the world. His art film, ***The Soul of Vinyl, Abbey Road Side 2***, screened at the 2016 New York City Independent Film Festival. Jim's film, ***The Case of the Deranged Sommelier*** won Best Experimental Film in the

2016 Directors Circle of Shorts Film Festival and the 2017 Lion's Head Film Festival. His film, **Still Mad as Hell**, screened at the 2017 New York City Independent Film Festival. His latest film, **It's Gonna Disappear**, screened at the 2021 New York Flash Film Festival.

Jim's education includes a Bachelor of Arts from The University of Texas at Austin, a Juris Doctor from Southern Methodist University in Dallas, and Level One Wine Sommelier Certification from the International Wine and Spirits Guild.